D0607909

Pictures and Stories from Forgotten Children's Books

DOVER *Pictorial Archive* SERIES

Pictures and Stories from Forgotten Children's Books

BY ARNOLD ARNOLD

Dover Publications, Inc., New York

Published in Canada by General Publishing Company, Ltd., 30 Lesmill Road, Don Mills, Toronto, Ontario.

Published in the United Kingdom by Constable and Company, Ltd., 10 Orange Street, London WC 2.

Pictures and Stories from Forgotten Children's Books is a new work, published for the first time by Dover Publications, Inc., in 1969.

Standard Book Number: 486-22041-9
Library of Congress Catalog Card Number: 77-86640

Manufactured in the United States of America
Dover Publications, Inc.
180 Varick Street
New York, N.Y. 10014

To Gail for all her patience,
shared interests and enthusiasm;
for her generosity
and for her love.

Contents

Pictures and Stories
from Forgotten Children's Books

Introduction

CHILDREN'S literature—books written and printed especially for the amusement of children—was almost entirely unknown prior to 1650. With a few exceptions it was nearly non-existent even one hundred years later. But the seeds had been sown.

Up to that time only the smallest fraction of the child population was required to learn reading and writing. For these few it was considered sufficient that they exercised their beginning skills by memorizing their catechism and by copying from hornbooks—bone and wood tablets inscribed with the alphabet.

If the child born before 1750 required further education, his scholastic diet consisted of reading and repeating moralistic orations and tracts, excerpted from adult lay and ecclesiastic writings. Once literate enough to take his place in commerce, he was forthwith apprenticed. If his station in life demanded more extensive academic training, he might graduate to endless studies of Greek and Roman texts in the original. Children, once past the swaddling stage, were regarded and treated as miniature, if recalcitrant, adults.

Those stories, fables and ditties with which children were familiar were mostly bowdlerized versions of the songs of troubadours of the Middle Ages, now a part of the oral tradition. These tales were still told by the fireside, most with a laborious moral attached.

Several separate influences brought about the birth of a distinct child literature in the eighteenth century. It is of course absurd to imagine clear beginnings in the stream of history. The origins of child literature can be found in trends and indications rather than in recognizable beginnings.

The first of these appears as the Puritan conviction that the child, conceived in sin, must be made aware of himself as the product of evil. He needed to be converted, preferably made ready for an early demise, in order to redeem himself, or meet his just rewards in hell. A forerunner of such a children's book was Erasmus's *Zuchtbüchlein*, or book of manners (Strasbourg, 1531). This was followed by the verses late in the seventeenth century of James Janeway, John Bunyan and, early in the eighteenth century, Isaac Watts.

The Egg's no Chick by falling from the Hen;
Nor man a Christian, till he's born agen . . . *

This vein continued into the next century, and also into this, the twentieth, as the Puritan spirit merged with the Victorian throughout Europe and America. In the early nineteenth century the names of authors like Mrs. Trimmer and Mrs. Sherwood cast long shadows as they marched across the nursery as if to

* John Bunyan, *A Book for Boys and Girls; or, Country Rhymes for Children*, 1686.

war against Fairies, Elves, Hobgoblins and other happy nonsense. They were supported in this battle by the Sunday School movement, started in England in 1775 by Robert Raikes, soon to be followed by the American Tract Society, and, among others, Samuel Griswold Goodrich, better known as Peter Parley. All these wagged their fingers in print, warning children against their own playful and imaginative natures.

The manipulative school of child literature has its counterpart in our day. Only the emphasis has changed. Then it was the moral tale, written at times in high-blown language, at others in words of one syllable only. Now this has been supplanted by the psychologically manipulative story in which the "Little Truck" always wins over the "Big Truck" and the "Little Train" always puffs into the station well ahead of the "Big Train." These also tend to be written according to formula and confining, anti-literate, age-grouped vocabularies.

It is useful to keep such comparisons in mind when reading some of the ponderous old stories and doggerel. Then as now there were few talented children's authors. It is obviously far easier to turn out stereotyped, dry moral tales than to invent imaginative and literate tales.

> The love of things rendered quaint and interesting by lapse of time and change of surroundings seems to grow on one imperceptibly. We have all wondered whether the elders who presented, and the children who read, these forgotten little books, recognized the unconscious humour of the writers of the text and the drawers of the pictures.*

* Andrew W. Tuer, *Pages and Pictures from Forgotten Children's Books*, Leadenhall Press, London, 1898–1899.

I do not wonder. I am quite sure that the purveyors of heavy-fisted rectitude were deadly serious, their justification being then, as now: "If it sells it has to be good."

The second stream of child-oriented books can be said to stem from Comenius's *Orbis sensualium pictus*, published in Germany in 1657 and translated into English one year later. This pictorial encyclopedia addressed itself exclusively to children and was designed to stimulate their curiosity and a larger view of the world. It is interesting that this children's book preceded by more than one hundred years the efforts of the French Encyclopedists—Rousseau, Diderot and others—to compile for adult readers all information then known. Comenius's *Orbis pictus* was reprinted, re-edited and pirated in hundreds of editions even late into the nineteenth century. It stimulated the concept of education through entertainment and subordinated text to illustration. This book or its genre may have inspired the movement of play-learning and sympathetic instruction that led from Pestalozzi to Froebel, Montessori to Dewey.

A third trend was the rediscovery of fable and fairy tale. *Aesop's Fables* had first been translated by Caxton into English in 1484. These, like La Fontaine's *Fables*, were not especially intended as reading matter for children. It has been, and will continue to be argued, that children of that day did see and read these fables, legends and tales which were primarily written and published for adults. Curious children, given the opportunity, have always ransacked the libraries of their elders. Enlightened, well-to-do parents undoubtedly did permit and encourage their children to read suitable adult books. But this was surely the exception rather than the rule, particularly in view of the rarity and cost of books of that day.

Perrault's *Tales of Mother Goose* (*Histoires ou contes du temps passé, avec les moralités*; *Les Contes de ma mère l'oie*, Paris, 1697) were the first fairy tales specially written and published for children. Whether this book was written by father or son is still a matter of debate among bibliophiles. In either case, Perrault, father or son, was the forerunner of the brothers Grimm, of Andersen, Halliwell, Andrew Lang and Alice Gomme, who gathered, and sometimes improvised on, the oral tradition. A new interest among litterateurs in the preservation of folklore and culture of the medieval past was astir, instead of exclusive preoccupation with Greek and Roman classics.

These legends survived the critical onslaught of the Puritans because it was then customary to attach a moral to each, no matter how farfetched or redundant. Perrault's "Little Red Riding Hood" ended with a warning to girls not to permit themselves to be picked up by wolves, a warning that is still good today. Aesop, included in the school curriculum even before the early eighteenth century, was also a victim of this tedious practice. Nevertheless fables and fairy tales, once they had fallen into the hands of children, became a favorite target of self-appointed custodians of public morality, such as Mrs. Sherwood and Goodrich.

Even today the fairy tale is under attack, though from another quarter. Now the objections are raised by psychiatrically oriented meddlers. Not long ago Little Red Riding Hood was attacked as being unsuitable in her original dress as potentially trauma-producing. Since then several publishers have edited this classic tale, excluding these supposed psychologically disturbing details. It is still the same old Calvinist hand, ever ready to prune literature and to whittle it down to its own withered size.

The fourth set of events that influenced the birth of a separate children's literature was that of mechanical improvements in printing techniques and papermaking. The printing trades in the middle of the eighteenth century were hardly changed from the time of Gutenberg. Henceforth industrial innovations in this, as in other fields, encouraged larger production at lesser cost. Initially the expanded potential created a proliferation of adult literature in the form of chapbooks. The stirring of the Industrial Revolution demanded greater literacy of the lower classes. It was to this market that publishers addressed themselves first. The chapbook reached segments of the population that had never before been able to afford print.

At the same time there appeared a new adult literature that, though it addressed itself to a sophisticated adult readership, soon found its way into the hands of children, and into the lower-class chapbook, though often in adulterated form. Typical of these books are Bunyan's *Pilgrim's Progress* (1684), Defoe's *Robinson Crusoe* (1719), Swift's *Gulliver's Travels* (1726), *The Arabian Nights*, *Baron Munchausen's Travels* (1785).

Almost the only printed matter that reached the lower classes before the seventeenth century consisted of what in France has been so aptly named *Imagerie Populaire*—popular pictures. These consisted of religious images, sometimes imprinted with psalms or prayers, sold outside the cathedral. In the eighteenth century these prints were converted into ballad sheets and prints describing topical events and folk tales.

The chapbook derives its name from "chapmen," wandering peddlars of novelties and gimcrackery who trudged from farm to hamlet to village, the length and breadth of England. These, though reference is made to them much earlier, achieved their greatest popularity from the late seventeenth to the early nineteenth centuries and had their counterparts in most other European countries.

> [In England, chapmen were licensed as] "Hawkers, Vendors, Pedlars, petty Chapmen, *and unruly people.*" In a major part of this country, and to the larger portion of its population, these little Chap-books were nearly the only mental pabulum offered. Their great variety adapted them for every purchaser, and they may be roughly classed under the following heads:—Religious, Diabolical, Supernatural, Superstitious, Romantic, Humorous, Legendary, Historical, Biographical, and Criminal. Favourites of the Romantic School were "Jack the Giant Killer," "Reynard the Fox," etc. . . . The Jestbooks, pure and simple, are, from their extremely coarse witticisms, utterly incapable of being reproduced for general reading nowadays, and the whole of them are more or less highly spiced; but even here were shades of humor to suit all classes, from the solemn foolery of the "Wise Men of Gotham," or the "World turned upside down," to the rollicking fun of "Tom Tram," "The Fryar and the Boy," or "Jack Horner." The old legends still held sway . . . "Robin Hood," "The Blind Beggar of Bethnal Green," and "The Children in the Wood."*

These were the springs from which flowed the material that merged into the stream of children's books as we know them today. James Cole (*ca.*1715), Thomas Boreman (*ca.*1740) and John Newbery, who first went into production in 1744, were probably the first to devote themselves exclusively to publication of books addressed to children. It is an amusing side light that John Newbery was also in the patent-medicine business, which may have contributed to his success as a publisher. He certainly knew that it paid to advertise, the dexterity acquired in one field serving handily in the other.

> This day was published Nurse Truelove's New Years Gift of the book of books for children, adorned with cuts, and designed as a present for every little boy who would become a great man, and ride upon a fine horse; and to every little girl who would become a great woman and ride in the lord-mayor's gilt coach. Printed for the author who has ordered these books to be given gratis to all boys and girls, at the Bible and Sun in St. Paul's Churchyard, they paying for the binding which is only twopence for each book.*

The more things change, the more they remain the same. Today many publishers, unable to compete with television for the adult audience, are vying with one another for the seemingly insatiable juvenile market. Like their forebears of two hundred years ago, they sometimes engage in questionable and deceptive promotional practices that were old when George III was young.

Newbery was succeeded by others. Such names as Benjamin Harris, a direct successor, competitors such as Marshall, Darton, Tabart & Co.; Newman & Dean;

* John Ashton, *Chap-Books of the Eighteenth Century*, Chatto & Windus, London, 1882, Introduction viii–xi.

* Advertisement by John Newbury, 1755.

as well as chapbook publishers Catnach, Rusher, and many others swelled the stream of British printer-publisher-booksellers. These copied one another, pirated text and cuts, occasionally wrote their own material and sometimes even commissioned authors to write for the burgeoning juvenile market.

Shortly after 1800 similar phenomena occurred in the United States. Here the publishing trade soon flourished, encouraged by the example of Benjamin Franklin. American publishers engaged in the same practices as their European cousins. They pirated from them and from each other, sometimes buying rights from British and German firms.

But the tide of piracy was soon reversed. In 1827 S. G. Goodrich published in the United States the first of his many "Peter Parley" books for children. In addition to seven million copies of authorized editions of 120 titles sold in the United States and abroad, countless others were pirated and sold in England.

Identical trends developed in Germany. In France the *Imagerie Populaire* turned from topical prints to children's cutouts and booklets. By 1820 the publishing trade received a great boost in production potential through the invention of lithography.

There are of course other, lesser influences that gave shape to children's literature. The medieval Bestiary led to the myriad of books for children about birds and beasts, some of the books instructive, others whimsical. Side lights of adult humor and fancy, the street cries of vendors, the Limerick, the riddle and conundrum and the rebus, the latter an adult fad of the eighteenth century, all seeped into the hands of children.

Most eighteenth-century children's books were printed in black, illustrated with woodcuts. By the end of the century part of each edition was sold colored by hand. Children in factories would paint onto sheets printed in black outline on a semi-production basis, one child brushing on red, another blue, and so on, according to precolored patterns. The invention of lithography—printing from stones—made the printing of large, multi-colored editions economically feasible. Those printers who were unable or unwilling to invest in color plates used stencils that were superimposed on black and white prints, one stencil for each color. A whole sheet could thus be profusely colored, each color applied by the sweep of a large brush. Later a mechanized stencil machine was developed, one of which is still in operation at the Imprimerie Pellerin at Épinal in Alsace-Lorraine. This company is probably the last remaining of its kind, a company which, since 1748, has seemed to sum up in its history the evolution of children's literature. Sad to tell, but in keeping with the time, this company is now almost exclusively devoted to comic-book production and the reproduction of facsimiles of their own early prints for decoration of plastic place mats and wastebaskets.

The writing and illustration of early children's books were mostly in the hands of hacks. Artists such as Bewick, the ingenious and talented wood engraver of the late eighteenth century, Blake, Doré and Cruikshank set standards that were only occasionally matched later in the century and even in this, the twentieth. Yet even the early crude illustrations, many taken directly from chapbooks, had a charm and childlike conception infinitely superior to the childish, condescending style of much of the surrounding text.

The content of many of these early children's books was unreal, filled with misinformation, prejudice and false ideals. It is a tribute to the children of that day that they managed to survive this diet of badly written and confusing literature. Some even grew into wise, kindly and literate adults. It gives hope for the children of today who must withstand an even greater barrage of corroding nonsense from mass communications media.

> The lady who thought it necessary to teach children that fishes have no legs, and who believed that sea-water when boiled becomes fresh probably did not follow literature for a livelihood.*

Yet such names as Oliver Goldsmith, Charles and Mary Lamb, Sir Walter Scott, Hans Christian Andersen, appear in increasing numbers in the late eighteenth and early nineteenth centuries. Some brought whimsy and imagination, others at least literary craftsmanship that resulted in the flowering of children's literature. It was the start of a tradition that led to James Fenimore Cooper, Poe, Lear, Marryat, Dickens, Carroll, Jules Verne, Twain, and R. L. Stevenson, among others.

This tradition remains with us still, side by side with the mountains of trashy mass-produced juveniles of the supermarket. Television and comic-book versions of the best of the classics may attempt to debase even these, but they cannot obliterate the originals. The originals remain as standards to be emulated rather than imitated by those writers of today and tomorrow who are touched by and can feel a kinship with the magic vision of childhood.

* Andrew W. Tuer, *Stories from Old-Fashioned Children's Books*, Leadenhall Press, London, 1899–1900.

The following pages are excerpted from my own collection of early children's books. These books are not necessarily the earliest editions. Some are reprints of earlier works. I leave the cataloguing to the librarian, the tracing of origins to the folklorist. This book is intended as a survey of the manner and literary and illustrative styles whereby children were introduced to culture and learning before 1850. I have made the selections, as I originally selected the books, not with the eye of the stamp collector who wishes to fill his album pages. Rather I have chosen whatever seems amusing and pertinent. Many of these selections can still be read to and with today's children, giving them a sense of kinship with history and sympathy for their great-great-great grandparents.

The selections are presented as they originally appeared, with all misspellings and other typographical crudities faithfully preserved.

This collection of books is divided into eleven chapters, each representing a particular genre. Within each chapter the texts are arranged in chronological order, except where juxtaposition of a later or earlier work makes for an interesting comparison. For example, Scott's poem "The Drum," an ardent pacifist plea, has been placed next to "The Story of the Little Drummer." The latter promotes a more warlike view, one that is still typically American: patriotic, but also very conscious of the dangers and discomforts of warfare. Both these works must be seen in historical context. "The Drum" was a protest against the "ravaged plains" of the Napoleonic Wars; "The Little Drummer" reflects the War of 1812.

I/ *Morals and Manners*

CHILDREN'S books throw much light on the temper of the times in which they appear, and those in this chapter all deal with the morals, manners and expected behavior of the period from 1750 to 1850. Punishment for the slightest transgression was swift, brutal and devastating, whether parental or divine. Such hell-fire-and-brimstone morality is now preached only by backwoods evangelists. Death, maiming and loss of senses inevitably follow hard on the heels of the slightest misdeed, and such retribution is often described in gleefully gory detail. The expressed morality is predominantly female. Boyish sport is frowned upon more often than not, and warned against, no matter how harmless. Many of the authors were females with pronounced ideas, long-forgotten childhoods and probably repressed adult lives. Their outlook was foreign to the ways of children. These points of view, inherited from Puritan days, greatly influenced Victorian values. The children's book was one of the pathways of transmission. It must also be kept in mind that the latter half of the eighteenth century was libertarian, rollicking and Hogarthian, a life from which these gentle women authors hoped to protect the young.

But the conflict between preachment and observable everyday life probably seemed no stranger to those children than the contradictions between professed and experienced morality in our own day. Perhaps these false standards are better than none, or superior to the peer-group morality which seems to be the prescription offered today's middle-class children.

Some of the products of this severe morality turned into the free-wheeling and hard-dealing merchants, manufacturers and robber barons of the latter half of the nineteenth century. Hence it is equally possible that today's children may, in protest against permissiveness, become stiff-necked moralists in their time.

Odd and often amusing side lights can be found in these little stories and poems, such as the conspiracy between mother and brother against "Louisa" in "The Remedy." Sibling rivalry crops up in classic form in "Pride Reproved" ("The Rosebud") and in "Put Down the Baby."

Urban street life was possibly even more hazardous than today, if judged by "Crossing Streets." Danger lurked everywhere, from kicking, biting horses and careening carriages, to flying spinning tops. Then there is the "she was poor but she was honest" theme of "Dolly Primrose," the silly farm girl who was robbed of all her belongings, or worse, in the evil enticing streets of London about 1800. Beggars infested the streets, similar to those who still haunt the tourist in Eastern countries. Charity had to be exercised with caution, as illustrated by "Give with Prudence" and "Fanny Overkind," so that excessive generosity would not cause gastric disturbances in the recipient.

But there are also more gentle, humorous and child-like views, as expressed in the "Good Boy's" and "Good Girl's" soliloquies. The text shown here is an American edition of the British original first published in London by William Darton, Jr., in 1811.

Here included is only one example of the "conversational style" prevalent in many of the early children's books. These were stories written in dialogue, usually between parents or teachers and the children in their charge. Most of these are endlessly tedious. However, the dialogue quoted from "Selling Slaves by the Pound" (*The Slave's Friend*, Vol. 1) shows yet another side of the moralist, one that was to take beneficial effect much later in the century.

The unlikely result of the "Cautious Mother's" literary pruning and censorship would be entertaining, were it not a forerunner of the attitude of busybody parent-teachers associations and super-patriots in our more recent history.

Finally there is the little volume of "Simple Stories for Little Folk," an American production, similar to many others on both sides of the Atlantic. Such books as this were written around woodcuts and engravings a printer-publisher might happen to have lying about his shop. Why else assemble such ill-assorted, unconsciously funny doggerel? Flexibility was the custom then, as it still is. Today the publisher merely changes and modernizes the cover in order to make use of old plates, selling his tired wares as modern merchandise. Such books as these, then as now, are merchandise rather than children's literature. *Caveat emptor*.

1 An Exchange of Letters

FROM NEWBERY'S FAMILIAR LETTER WRITER, ADAPTED TO THE CAPACITIES OF YOUNG PEOPLE

London: Printed for E. Newbery, the Corner of St. Paul's Churchyard, 1788

Letter from a Young Gentleman to His Companion, Recovered from a Fit of Sickness

It gives me the most sincere pleasure to hear, that my dear Tommy is recovering his health so rapidly. Had you died, it would have been to me a most terrible loss; but it has pleased God to preserve my friend. I will take the first opportunity that offers to call and tell you how valuable your life is to

Your sincere friend and playfellow

Answer to the Preceding Letter

Your obliging letter, my dear Billy, is a fresh proof of your friendship and esteem for me. I thank God I am now perfectly recovered. I am in some doubt whether I ought not to consider my late illness as a just punishment for my crime of robbing Mr. Goodman's orchard, breaking his boughs, and spoiling his hedges. However, I am fully determined that no such complaints shall evermore come against,

Your sincere friend and playfellow

Illustrations from "The Gift of Friendship," New Haven (top), and "Watts' Divine Songs," New Haven, 1824 (bottom).

2 Watts' Divine Songs

New-Haven: Published by J. Babcock and Son, and S. Babcock and Co., 329 King-St., Charleston, S.C.; Sidney's Press, 1824

Against Quarrelling and Fighting

LET dogs delight to bark and bite,
  For God hath made them so;
Let bears and lions growl and fight,
  For 'tis their nature to.

BUT children, you should never let
  Such angry passions rise;
Your little hands were never made
  To tear each others' eyes.

LET love through all your actions run,
  And all your words be mild;
Live like the blessed virgin's Son,
  That sweet and lovely child.

Love between Brothers and Sisters

WHATEVER brawls disturb the street,
There should be peace at home;
Where sisters dwell and brothers meet,
Quarrels should never come.

BIRDS in their little nests agree,
And 'tis a shameful sight,
When children of one family,
Fall out and chide and fight.

HARD names at first and threat'ning words,
That are but noisy breath,
May grow to clubs and naked swords,
To murder and to death.

Innocent Play

ABROAD in the meadows, to see the young lambs
Run sporting about by the side of their dams,
With fleeces so clean and so white;
Or a nest of young doves, in a large open cage,
When they play all in love, without anger or rage,
How much may we learn from the sight!

IF we had been ducks, we might dabble in mud,
Or dogs, we might play till it ended in blood,
So foul and so fierce are their natures;
But Thomas, and William, and such pretty names,
Should be cleanly and harmless as doves, or as lambs,
Those lovely sweet innocent creatures.

3 The Nursery Garland

BEING A SELECTION OF SHORT POEMS, ADAPTED TO VERY EARLY YOUTH; COMPILED BY DR. MAVOR

J. Harris, London, 1806, second edition

Obedience to Parents

LET children that would fear the Lord
Hear what their teachers say;
With rev'rence meet their parent's word,
And with delight obey.

HAVE you not heard what dreadful plagues
Are threaten'd by the Lord,
To him that breaks his father's law,
Or mocks his mother's word?

WHAT heavy guilt upon him lies!
How cursed is his name!
The ravens shall pick out his eyes,
And eagles eat the same.

BUT those who worship God, and give
Their parents honours due,
Here on this earth they long shall live,
And live hereafter too.

WATTS

The Advantages of Early Religion

HAPPY the child whose tender years
Receive instructions well;
Who hates the sinner's path, and fears
The road that leads to hell.

WHEN we devote our youth to God,
'Tis pleasing in his eyes;
A flower, when offer'd in the bud,
Is no vain sacrifice.

'TIS easier work, if we begin
To fear the Lord betimes;
While sinners that grow old in sin
Are harden'd in their crimes.

LET the sweet work of pray'r and praise
Employ my youngest breath;
Thus I'm prepar'd for longer days,
Or fit for early death.

WATTS

The Drum

I HATE that Drums discordant sound,
Parading round, and round, and round:
To thoughtless youth it pleasure yields,
And lures from cities and from fields,
To sell their liberty for charms
Of tawdry lace and glitt'ring arms;
And when ambition's voice commands,
To march, and fight, and fall, in foreign lands.

I HATE that drum's discordant sound,
Parading round, and round, and round:
To me it talks of ravag'd plains,
And burning towns, and ruin'd swains,
And mangled limbs, and dying groans,
And widows' tears, and orphans' moans;
And all that Misery's hand bestows,
To swell the catalogue of human woes.

SCOTT

4 Story of the Little Drummer

FROM THE PRETTY PRIMER (THE JUVENILE GEM)

Huestis & Cozans, 104 Nassau Street, New York, circa 1825

2 THE LITTLE DRUMMER

LITTLE DICK leaving his home

DICK was the name of a little boy whose mother was very poor and had to work hard for something to eat. Little Dick had no work to do, and he often wished he could earn something to help his poor mother.

As Dick was walking about one day he saw a company of soldiers who were going to fight for their country; and being a brave little fellow, he thought he would join them:

THE LITTLE DRUMMER. 3

but as he was too small to carry a gun, he became a drummer, and bidding his poor mother good by, he marched away.

LITTLE DICK with his drum

Dick was very much pleased with his red jacket and new drum and thought it was a fine thing to be a soldier; but he soon got very tired and wanted to lie down, for he had marched all day in the hot sun, and was very tired and hungry.

At last the soldiers stopped, and after eating a cold supper they laid down on

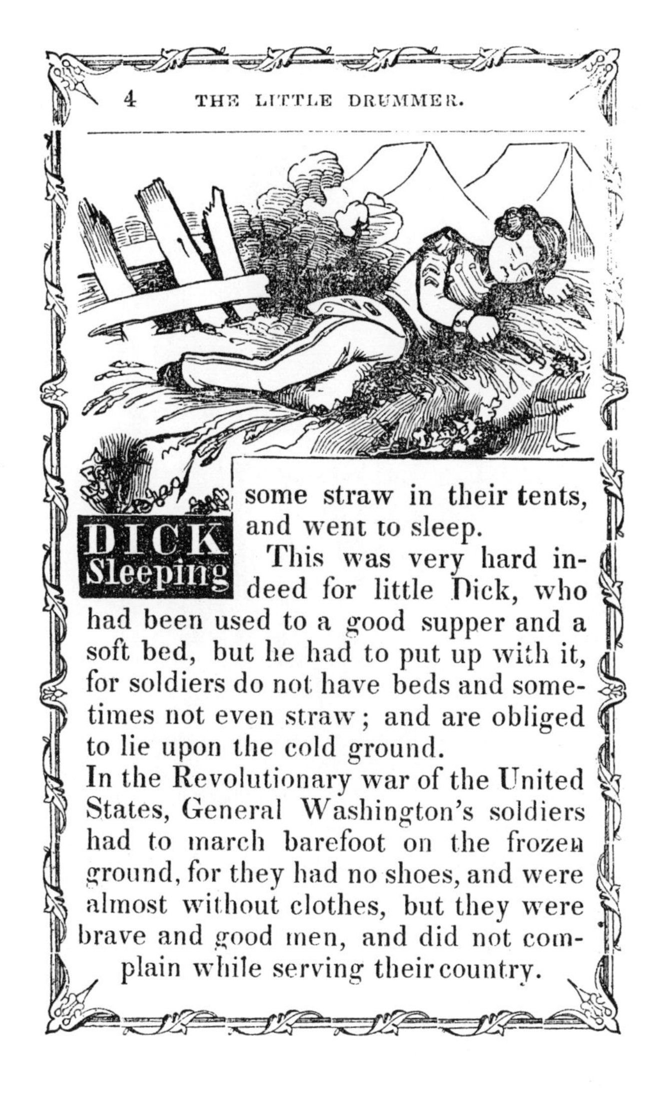

4 THE LITTLE DRUMMER.

DICK Sleeping

some straw in their tents, and went to sleep.

This was very hard indeed for little Dick, who had been used to a good supper and a soft bed, but he had to put up with it, for soldiers do not have beds and sometimes not even straw; and are obliged to lie upon the cold ground.

In the Revolutionary war of the United States, General Washington's soldiers had to march barefoot on the frozen ground, for they had no shoes, and were almost without clothes, but they were brave and good men, and did not complain while serving their country.

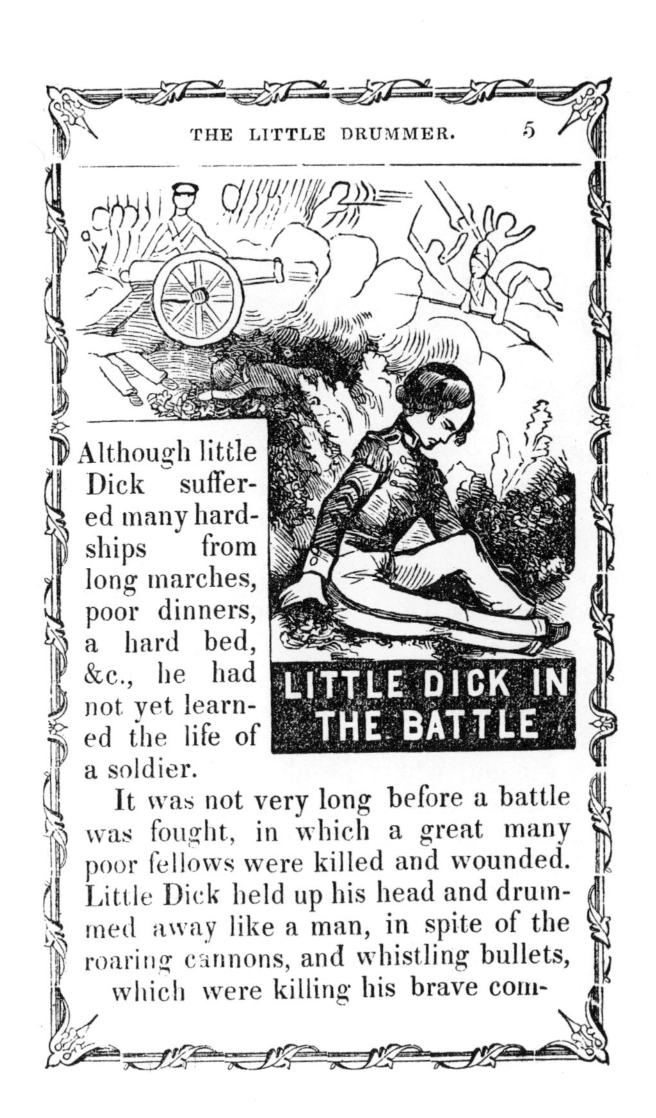

THE LITTLE DRUMMER. 5

LITTLE DICK IN THE BATTLE

Although little Dick suffered many hardships from long marches, poor dinners, a hard bed, &c., he had not yet learned the life of a soldier.

It was not very long before a battle was fought, in which a great many poor fellows were killed and wounded. Little Dick held up his head and drummed away like a man, in spite of the roaring cannons, and whistling bullets, which were killing his brave com-

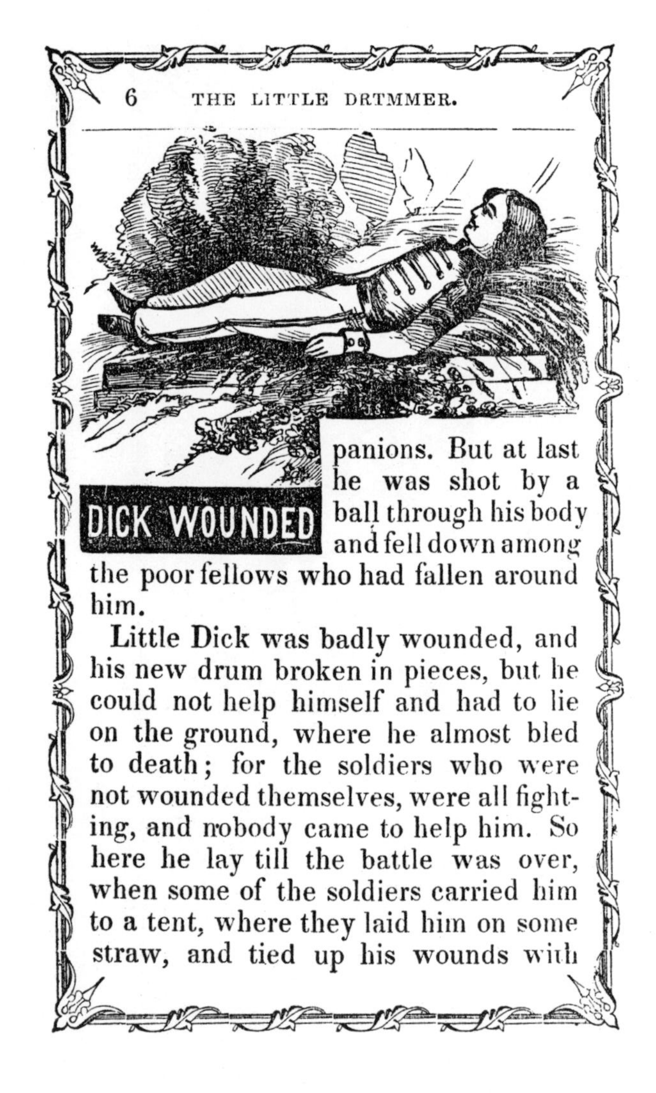

6 THE LITTLE DRTMMER.

DICK WOUNDED

panions. But at last he was shot by a ball through his body and fell down among the poor fellows who had fallen around him.

Little Dick was badly wounded, and his new drum broken in pieces, but he could not help himself and had to lie on the ground, where he almost bled to death; for the soldiers who were not wounded themselves, were all fighting, and nobody came to help him. So here he lay till the battle was over, when some of the soldiers carried him to a tent, where they laid him on some straw, and tied up his wounds with

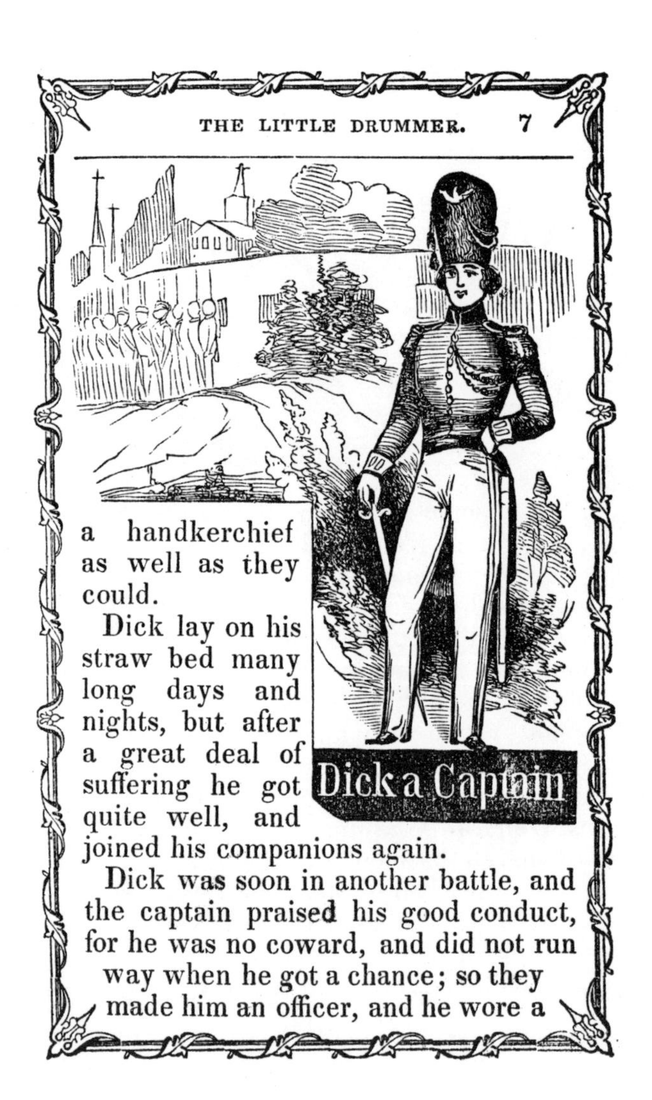

THE LITTLE DRUMMER. 7

Dick a Captain

a handkerchief as well as they could.

Dick lay on his straw bed many long days and nights, but after a great deal of suffering he got quite well, and joined his companions again.

Dick was soon in another battle, and the captain praised his good conduct, for he was no coward, and did not run way when he got a chance; so they made him an officer, and he wore a

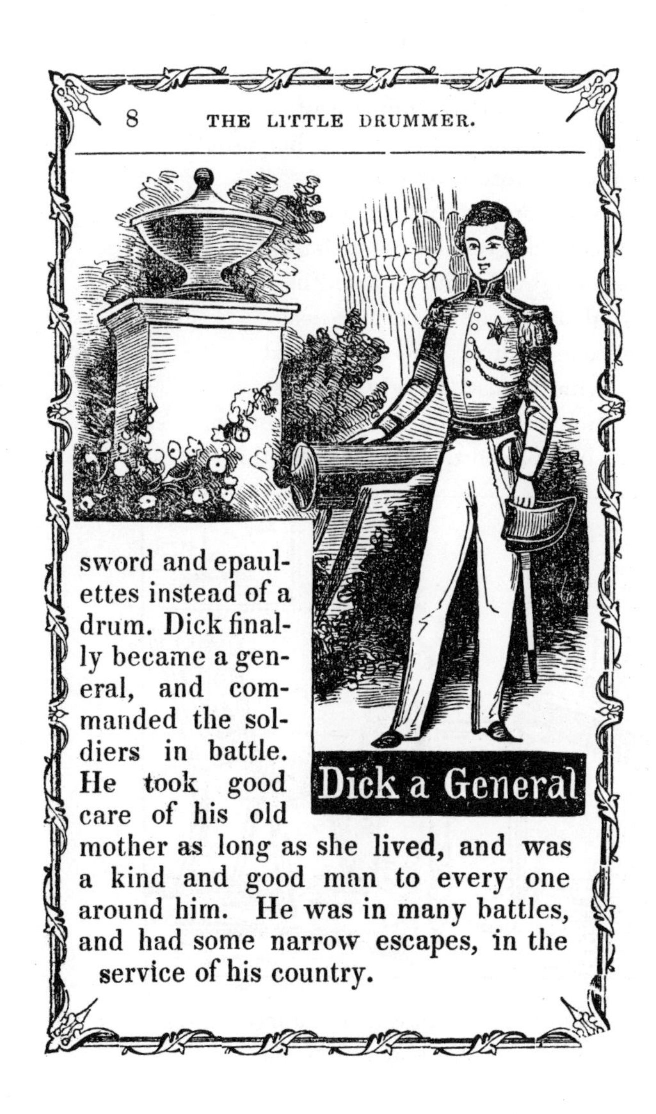

8 THE LITTLE DRUMMER.

sword and epaulettes instead of a drum. Dick finally became a general, and commanded the soldiers in battle. He took good care of his old mother as long as she lived, and was a kind and good man to every one around him. He was in many battles, and had some narrow escapes, in the service of his country.

Illustrations from "Rural Scenes," Cooperstown, 1839 (top); "The Little Scholar's Mirror," London, 1812 (middle); "Guess Again," Philadelphia, 1840 (bottom).

5 The Remedy

FROM THE LILY: A BOOK FOR CHILDREN: CONTAINING TWENTY-TWO TRIFLES IN VERSE ADORNED WITH CUTS

The lily loves the humble vale
and reads a silent moral tale.

London: Printed for J. Harris, St. Paul's Church-Yard, 1808

The Remedy

LOUISA was a pretty child,
Her temper flexible and mild.
She learnt her lessons all with ease,
And very seldom failed to please.
But still Louisa had a fault:
So fond of tasting sugar, salt,
Or anything, in short, to eat,
Puddings, pies, or wine or meat;
And as she was so often sick,
Mamma soon guessed the foolish trick,
And, planning for her little daughter,
By stratagem she fairly caught her. . . .
The dinner done, one winter's day,
And guests removed, their cards to play,
Louisa stole where they'd deserted,
And by her usual pranks diverted,
Here see this foolish, greedy lass
Draining the bottom of each glass, . . .
When, lo, a tumbler caught her sight,
Which gave Louisa new delight,
For it appeared half full of wine,
So sparkling, and so clear and fine,
She drank it quick, and hardly tasted,
Nor one drop of the liquor wasted.
Had you at that moment seen her face,
So much distorted by grimace,
How she stamped and cried and spluttered
Complained, grew sick, and faintly muttered,
Then sought the nursery and her bed;
And glad thereon to lay her head,
You soon, I think, had understood
The wine Louisa thought so good,
Was mixed with physic by her mother,
And slyly placed there by her brother.

AND from the sickness she endured
Her love of tasting soon was cured.

6 Juvenile Dialogues

OR RECREATIONS FOR SCHOOL BOYS, DURING THEIR LEISURE HOURS AT BOARDING SCHOOL. BY BILLY MERRYTHOUGHT

Chelmsford: Printed and Sold by I. Marsden, circa 1810

Wise Sayings for Children

NEVER be weary of well doing.

AS good sit still, as rise up and fall.

THE weakest goes to the wall.

ONE bad sheep will infect a flock.

Sam and Nat

SAM. Do not vex me.
NAT. Do I vex you?
SAM. Yes, you do.
NAT. How do I vex you?
SAM. You say pop, mop, Sam slop keeps a shop.
NAT. Does that vex you?
SAM. Yes, it does.
NAT. Then I will say so no more.

Mamma and Miss Ann

MAMMA. Go and buy a Toy, Ann.
ANN. I can buy a gun.
MAMMA. A gun is not fit for you, Ann.
ANN. Why is not a gun fit for me?
MAMMA. A gun is only fit for a boy.
ANN. May I buy a top?
MAMMA. No, but you may buy a mop.

7 The Dangers of the Streets

FROM TALES UNITING INSTRUCTION WITH AMUSEMENT: CONSISTING OF THE DANGERS OF THE STREETS; AND THROWING SQUIBS. ORNAMENTED WITH ENGRAVINGS

London: Printed for J. Harris, successor to E. Newbery, at the Original Juvenile Library, the corner of St. Paul's Churchyard

EDWARD AND GEORGE MANLY were brothers. Edward was nine years old, very sensible and prudent for his age, and as cautious in walking the streets of London as a man of forty. . . .

His brother George, who was about a year younger than he, was of a very different disposition. He was thoughtless and giddy, would run across streets when carriages were driving up at full speed, and often very narrowly escaped being run over. . . .

But see the dreadful consequences of his giddiness and folly! His foot slipped; he fell under the loaded waggon; the wheel passed over one of his legs, and shattered it in a most shocking manner.

Thus mangled and racked with pain, he shrieked most piteously and repented of his folly when too late. He was taken up by his brother and some charitable persons of the neighbourhood who laid him on his back upon a window shutter and carried him home in that manner crying and lamenting all the way.

His father sent in haste for a surgeon: the surgeon immediately came, examined his leg and found it so terribly shattered that he declared he could not cure it but must cut it entirely off at the knee.

George now roared worse than before at the thought of losing his leg. However, as nothing else could be done to save his life, he was forced to submit. The surgeon took out his instruments, cut the flesh all round with a sharp knife, cut through the bone with a saw, and thus poor George's leg was taken completely off. . . .

At length a wooden leg was made for him: with that he now hobbles about as well as he can; and at every step he repents of his giddiness and says to himself, "Ah, how cautious children ought to be in walking the streets!"

8 Dangerous Sports

A TALE ADDRESSED TO CHILDREN WARNING THEM AGAINST WANTON, CARELESS OR MISCHIEVOUS EXPOSURE TO SITUATIONS FROM WHICH ALARMING INJURIES SO OFTEN PROCEED. BY JAMES PARKINSON

London: Printed for H. D. Symonds, Paternoster Row, by Law & Gilbert, St. John's Square, Clerkenwell, 1808

IT IS NOT necessary to mount a horse to be exposed to danger from him since several children have had their skulls beat to pieces from the kick of a horse, in consequence of their sillily plucking the hairs of its tail. . . . So ferocious are they sometimes, that two dreadful instances have occurred lately; in one of which the hand of a gentleman was seized by a horse and terribly ground by his teeth. In the other, an enraged horse seized the arm of a poor man which he did not loosen until the bystanders had broken the bone of his nose by beating him; and the arm was so injured as to be obliged to be cut off. . . .

A young gentleman passing a dog slightly touched it with a switch he carried in his hand, upon which the ferocious animal turned and seized him; and in spite of the exertions of those around him continued his hold until the bowels of the youth appeared at the wound: I need hardly say that the poor youth died within a few hours. . . .

Never leave your penknife open, especially on a desk, since being likely to glide down, it may fall with its point into your thigh, or wound you just by the inner ankle, where the artery runs very near the surface. . . .

Never stand opposite to anyone who is spinning his top, nor sufficiently near to his side to receive it on your head should it hang in the string.

A foolish practice is that of jumping unnecessarily from high places; this is frequently done without the idea of any danger: but consider when you alight on your feet after such a jump with how severe a shock you meet the ground. Frequently by this shock is one of the bones of the legs broken, and even when this is not the case, the shock affects the ends of the bones at the knee or hip-joint so severely that their surfaces polished like glass, sustain very considerable injury; from which such diseases follow as may occasion the loss of a limb or of life. . . .

Think before you taste, and taste before you swallow. For want of attending to this simple rule I knew two poor children lose their lives. One from thoughtlessly tasting something he found in a bottle, and which was aqua fortis had his mouth and throat so burnt that he died in the greatest agonies. The other was a little girl, who playing alone in a parlour, perceived a bottle of liquor standing on the sideboard. On tasting the liquor she found it pleasant, and putting her mouth to the bottle drank so freely that when her mother came into the room she found her senseless on the floor. The liquor she had drank was brandy, and in a very few hours she died.

9 Dolly Primrose, The Dairy Maid

OR THE ILL EFFECTS OF ROVING: FROM DOLLY PRIMROSE, AND OTHER ENTERTAINING TALES

Publisher unknown, circa 1810

DOLLY PRIMROSE, a pretty young girl that lived as dairy maid at a farm-house in Berkshire, had heard much talk of London, and took it into her silly head that go she would, and get a service in town—"And who knows," said the foolish girl, "but I may return a fine lady."

Well, to London she went in the waggon, but had soon reason to repent her folly, for she stood gaping about with her bundle under her arm, wondering at every thing she saw, a very smart gentleman came up to her, and asked her kindly what she was looking for, and if he could render her any service? "Yes indeed, sir," answered the simpleton, "that is what I want; I came to London to seek a service, mayhap you can tell of one." "That I can, my pretty maid," said he, "come with me; I will take care of you—you shall want for nothing."

Away they went together, through bye-alleys and lonely streets, till poor Dolly began to get tired, which the gentleman perceiving, very kindly took the bundle, and said he would carry it for her; this she thought very good-natured in him, and thanked him accordingly; but all at once, at the corner of a dark passage, the good natured gentleman and bundle disappeared.

Doll made a great noise in the streets, and raised a mob about her, at which she was more frightend. By great good chance the waggoner that brought her to London, happing to pass that way on some business, knew her and went to her relief. Poor Doll went back the next day into the country, and got laughed at for her folly, besides the los of all her cloaths and money, and pain from the treatment of the mob.

Had Doll been contented, and staid at home, like a good and sober girl, she would not have been made the scoff and derision of all the country round.

Many simple and foolish people believe if they can get to London their fortunes are made; but they do not consider what a number of bad people there are there who make it their business to lead astray the ignorant and unwary, and indeed it is a sad but a known truth that many live by such wicked and abominable practices.

My little reader will do well to consider that whoever takes to a roving life expose themselves to a variety of temptations and difficulties, which, while they are living with their parents and friends they have no idea of.

The Accident

The Faithful Dog

Trifle Not

Imprudence

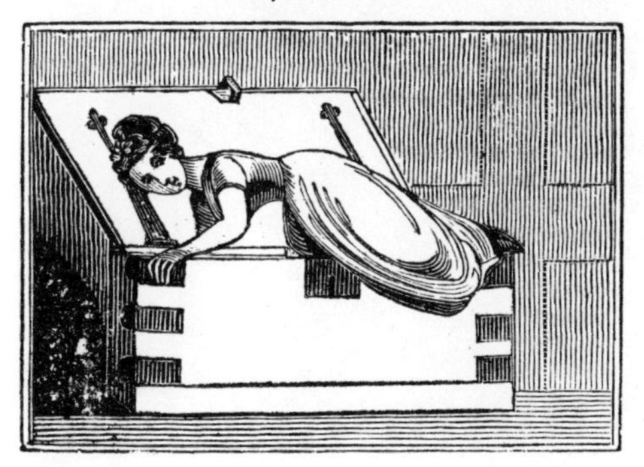

All illustrations on this page are from "The Little Scholar's Mirror," London, 1812.

10 My Sister

BY MARY BELSON

Publisher unknown, circa 1820

YET when I sought to kill a fly
Who then to save its life would try
And say 'twas cruel to make it die?
MY SISTER

WHO saw me mount the Rocking Horse
And then stood by, to check its course,
Lest her dear boy should get a toss?
MY SISTER

WHEN infant-like, I broke your toys,
Who saw them fall, and heard the noise,
Yet would not spoil my baby joys?
MY SISTER

AND when I snatch'd her new wax doll,
Making it o'er the carpet roll,
Who suffer'd it, without control?
MY SISTER

WHEN up the Ladder I would go,
(How wrong it was, I now well know)
Who cried, but held it fast below?
MY SISTER

ONCE too I threw my top too far,
It touch'd thy cheek, and left a scar?
Who tried to hide it, from Mamma.
MY SISTER

11 The Good Boy's Soliloquy

CONTAINING HIS PARENTS' INSTRUCTIONS, RELATIVE TO HIS DISPOSITION AND MANNERS

New York: Published by Samuel Wood & Sons, No. 261, Pearl-Street; and Samuel S. Wood & Co., No. 212, Market-st., Baltimore, 1822

The things my parents bid me do,
Let me attentively pursue.

To the Reader

I TAKE the liberty, my dear little Reader, of troubling you with the present address, in order to request a favour, which I hope you will be kind enough to grant, in return for the pleasure and profit, of which it has been my endeavour to make THE GOOD BOY'S SOLILOQUY the vehicle.

The favour which I solicit, is, that you will seriously practise the advice which I give you: doing all that I command, and avoiding all that I censure; as otherwise, instead of obtaining the character, to which I aspire, of a prudent and salutary monitor, I shall, on the contrary, be accused of putting a number of naughty things into your head, which it is most probable you never think of yourself.

As, I dare say, you are now impatient to proceed to the SOLILOQUY itself, I shall only detain you to observe, that you must consider it as spoken in your own person, and the name, at the conclusion, as representing your own name; and, consequently, that you may change Richard Roe, into John Doe, John O Nokes, Peter Stiles, or any other. If you can adapt the rhyme in the foregoing line to such change, so much the better; but if not, you will only experience a disappointment to which we rhymers are frequently subject.

THE AUTHOR

THE things my parents bid me do,
Let me attentively pursue;
The things they bid me leave undone,
Let me essay as much to shun;
And that I may the better learn
Their will at all times to discern,
Let me their precepts now rehearse
In memory-refreshing verse.

THEY do not bid me mind my book,
For in it I delight to look;
They do not bid me mind my writing,
For it I also take delight in;
But mind the following directions,
If I would gain their good affections.

THE first, are sentiments of weight,
On which I oft should meditate.

THEY bid me practice love to all,
Both rich and poor, both great and small,
And never with resentment burn,
But good for evil still return;
I must abhor to swear or lie;
I must not have a scornful eye.
I must abhor to steal or wrong;
I must not have a railing tongue.
I must to generous acts incline,
And not desire what is not mine;
For 'tis as I should well believe,
Better to give than to receive.
I must not hurt or kill a fly,
For it can feel as well as I:
And I cannot, at will, repay,
The life which once I take away.

I now to lighter themes proceed;
But such as still attention need.

THEY bid me blow and wipe my nose,
And not to soil or tear my clothes;
But as a decent boy should do,
Preserve them long as good as new.
They bid me awkward tricks forbear,
And not to squint, or frown, or stare;
Or, spite of frequent reprimands,
Appear with dirty face or hands.
I must at meals be seasonable,
And must not lean upon the table,
I must not let my victuals drop,
Or spill my drink and make it slop.
I must not dip, howe'er I wish,
My spoon or finger in a dish;
Or entertain the dog or cat,
With dainty bits of skin or fat.

I must beware of the tea-urn,
And not presume the cock to turn;
Lest I should want sufficient cunning,
To stop it while profusely running;
And so be the unlucky elf
To flood the tray or scald myself.
I must, when from confinement free,
Discreetly use my liberty.
I must not bawl or make a noise,
I must not throw about my toys;
Or, with more glee than I could make 'em
To see what is within 'em, break 'em.
I must not break about my bread,
And then upon the fragments tread,
Or squeeze it in my hands, or pick it,
And in a hole or cranny stick it.
I must not ugly faces scrawl
With charcoal, on a white-wash'd wall;

Or, as from room to room I walk,
Adorn them with designs in chalk.

I must not take away a knife,
As I would shun domestic strife;
To litter every place with chips,
Or cut my finger if it slips.

I must not ramble in the street,
Or play with every boy I meet.
I must not raise a dust for game,
Or water with a syringe aim.
I must not scamper in the mire,
Or fry the snow upon the fire.
I must not blow the candle out,
Or throw the smutty snuff about.
I must not gnaw or bite my nails;
I must not ride upon the rails.
I must not swing or clap the door;
I must not tumble on the floor.

I must not dirty the clean stairs;
I must not trample on the chairs.

I must not strike, I must not kick.
I must not throw a stone or stick.

I must not quarrel with the maid
When getting from or into bed;
But try to give her no delay,
And thank her as she goes away.
I must, in short, from morn till night,
Endeavour to do what is right;
And as much, the whole day long,
Endeavour to avoid what's wrong;
And hence, I should the better grow,
As long as I am RICHARD ROE.

12 The Good Girl's Soliloquy

CONTAINING HER PARENTS' INSTRUCTIONS, RELATIVE TO HER DISPOSITION AND MANNERS

New-York: Published by Samuel Wood & Sons, No. 261, Pearl-Street; and Samuel S. Wood & Co., No. 212, Market-st., Baltimore, 1820

WISE precepts have my parents taught,
To guide each action, word and thought:
Let me these precepts recollect,
And pay to each its due respect.

First, I must try to bear in mind,
That God is holy, just, and kind,
And that my thoughts and actions lie
Exposed to his all-seeing eye.
I must not take his name in vain,
Nor be in any sense profane;
I must obey my parents' word,
If I would wish to please the Lord—
Present or absent, do their will,
And love and reverence them still.

My fellow-creatures I must love;
By kindness my affection prove.
I must repeat the faults of none,
But look within and cure my own;
I must confess when I've done wrong,
Nor let a lie defile my tongue.

Whatever I engage to do,
I must at all events pursue.
All vulgar words I must detest,
Nor speak a dirty phrase in jest.

I must not steal—'tis awful sin!
Nor cheat my play-mates of a pin.
If I am rich I must not vaunt,
Nor scorn the humble sons of want—
Since God can give the wealth I prize
To those whom I had dar'd despise.
I must content and thankful be
With what he kindly grants to me.
I never must be vain in dress,
Nor grudge what others may possess—
For he who made both great and small,
Gives what he pleases to us all.

If others need what I can spare,
I must with them my treasures share—
A portion cheerfully impart,
And not indulge a stingy heart.
My time I must not idly waste,
Since all my hours fly off in haste—
But each new minute strive to fill
With some new acts of duty still.

MY *manners*, too must be mending
In smaller things, though worth attending.

I must not pout when I am chid,
Nor whine in doing what I'm bid;
Nor contradict, nor snatch away
The toys, when I with children play;

Nor make wry faces in a pet,
To cause a lesser child to fret.
I must not slap, nor pinch, nor bite,
Nor do a single thing in spite;
Nor whistle, shout, or jump like boys,
To vex the family with noise;
I must not tell what's said or done
In families, to any one—
For then I should deserve the shame
That fixes on a tattler's name.
I must not my own praises seek,
Nor interrupt when others speak—
And raise my voice with earnest tone,
As if I must be heard alone.
I must not sit in others' places,
Nor sneeze, nor cough in people's faces;
Nor with my fingers pick my nose,
Nor wipe my hands upon my clothes.
And if I would be truly neat,
I never must my breakfast eat
Till I have comb'd and brush'd my hair,
And wash'd my face and hands with care.

At meals I must not be too nice
In seeking for a dainty slice;
Nor ask for pudding, fowl or fish,
When there's but little in the dish.
Nor fill my mouth, till I'm unable
To speak, when spoken too, at table;
Nor stick my elbows out too wide,
And hit the person at my side;
Nor loll, nor yawn, nor sit uncouth,
Nor take the cloth to wipe my mouth.
When I am eating bread or fruits,

Or any thing my palate suits,
If I have more than I desire,
I must not throw it in the fire—

The morsel which I do not need,
Might a young bird or chicken feed.
What any creature could enjoy,
I must not wantonly destroy.
And every night I must reflect,
If I've been guilty of neglect
Of any practice recommended,
And for my benefit intended.
And if I find I am to blame,
I must acknowledge it with shame,
And to my heavenly Father pray,
To make me better every day,
Till I am fit to dwell on high,
Where faithful children never die.

13 The Results of Stealing a Pin

FROM THE RANKS IN LIFE, FOR THE AMUSEMENT AND INSTRUCTION OF YOUTH

London: J. Drury, 36 Lombard Street, corner of Plough Court, 1821

A LAD when at school, one day stole a pin,
And said that no harm was in such a small sin,
He next stole a knife, and said 'twas a trifle;
Next thing he did was pockets to rifle,
Next thing he did was a house to break in,
The next thing—upon a gallows to swing.
So let us avoid all little sinnings,
Since such is the end of petty beginnings.

14 The Cautious Mother

FROM JUVENILE ANECDOTES, FOUNDED ON FACTS, COLLECTED FOR THE AMUSEMENT OF CHILDREN BY PRISCILLA WAKEFIELD

London: Harvey & Darton, 55 Gracechurch Street, 1825, seventh edition

THERE are few books so pure in sentiment and expression as to be completely unexceptionable: even many of the publications that have been written expressly for youth, are defaced by exclamations, inconsistent with that simplicity which is the chief ornament of an unperverted mind. Mrs. Dennis was so particular with respect to the books she admitted amongst her children, that it was her constant practice to examine the most childish story-book, before she permitted them to read it; and as she considered instruction as the chief object in reading, she never scrupled to sacrifice the beauty of a new purchase, by freely cutting out as many leaves as contained passages likely to give them false ideas, or to corrupt their innocence. So very exact was she in her correctness, that not an objectionable sentence escaped. Thus there were but few books in the library of her school-room, that did not bear the marks of her hand. The children, believing their mamma to be wiser than any person whatever, and being assured also that her love for them induced her to take this trouble, showed no desire to see those parts which she had effaced. In time they became so accustomed to her alterations, that they omitted the words through which she had drawn a line, as a thing in course. . . .

At about seven years of age, she was obliged to relinquish Theodosius, her eldest boy, to the care of a gentleman who was engaged in the education of a few scholars. Mr. Perrin, not supposing him to be well qualified, gave him a spelling-book by way of trial; but he presently found that he was capable of reading something of a superior kind; upon which he took another book from the shelf, and, making an apology for having offered him a lesson so much beneath his powers, desired him to read a speech in one of Madame Genlis' Dramas. The little boy began in a manner that convinced Mr. Perrin that the utmost diligence and judgment had been exerted, to prepare him for his future progress in more difficult studies. After advancing to the middle of the page, he suddenly stopped, and looking up with great innocency at Mr. Perrin, said, "Pray, Sir, where is your pencil?" "What occasion can you have for a pencil, my dear, whilst you are engaged in your lesson?" "Do not you see, Sir," said the little boy, "that there is the awful name which I dare not repeat; and my mamma used always to draw a line through those words which she did not choose we should say." Mr. Perrin apprehended his meaning in a moment, and complied with his request. The custom pleased him so well, that he adopted it ever after in those books which he appointed for the use of his scholars.

15 Little Rhymes for Little Folks

Published by M. Day & Co., New York, circa 1830

The Rocking-Horse

WHEN Charles has done reading
His book every day,
Then he goes with his hoop
In the garden to play;

OR, his whip in his hand,
Quickly mounts up across,
And then gallops away
On his fine rocking-horse.

Little Fanny

SO Fanny, my love,
You've a pretty new frock,
I wish you your health, dear, to wear it;
'Tis so very neat,
And it fits you so well,
You'll be careful, I hope, not to tear it.

Tom Twig

ONCE little Tom Twig he went to a fair,
And what did he do the while he was there?
Little Tom Twig bought a fine bow and arrow,
And what did he shoot? Why a poor little sparrow.
Oh fie, little Tom! with your fine bow and arrow,
How cruel to shoot at a poor little sparrow!

Boys at Play

PRAY my good dame,
Can you tell any news?
Two little boys playing
Without any shoes;

OH fie, little boys,
You will make nursey scold,
And both be laid up
With a very bad cold.

James and His Mother

MOTHER I want to take a ride to-day,
Says James one morning fine,
My horse is ready at the door,
If thou to it incline.

MY son, I fear the horse will run,
And throw thee off, my dear,
Do give it up, and stay at home,—
My heart is filled with fear.

JAMES had better mind his mother,
And try ever hard to please her.

16 The Two Sisters

FROM THE PRETTY PRIMER (THE JUVENILE GEM)

Huestis & Cozans, 104 Nassau Street, New York, circa 1825

2 THE SISTERS.

THE SISTERS

There once was, two
Sweet little girls
Named Margaret and Kate,
And every day
They went to school,
And never went too late.

THE SISTERS. 3

Going to School

Their mother, she
Was kind to them,
And wished them to obey;
She always sent them
Both to school,
And told them not to play.

4 THE SISTERS.

STOPPING TO PLAY

But once they met
Some other girls,
Who stopp'd awhile to play,
And made a little
Baby house,
Where they might spend the day.

THE SISTERS. 5

GOING TO SLEEP

The school was out,
They all went home,
For night was coming fast;
But these two girls
Who stopped to play,
Both fell asleep at last.

6
THE SISTERS.
THEIR MOTHER
Their mother wondered
Where they were,
And looked and looked each way,
She thought that they
Were coming home,
And might have lost their way.

THE SISTERS.
7
LOOKING FOR THEM
So she put on
Her hat and shawl,
And after them did go;
The night was dark,
The rain did fall,
And loud the wind did blow.

17 The Snow-Drop

A COLLECTION OF RHYMES FOR THE NURSERY BY THE AUTHORS OF "ORIGINAL POEMS," EMBELLISHED WITH BEAUTIFUL ENGRAVINGS

New-Haven: Printed and published by S. Babcock, circa 1820

The Little Child

I'M a very little child,
Only just have learned to speak:
So I should be very mild,
Very tractable and meek.

IF my dear mamma were gone,
  I should perish soon, and die,
When she left me all alone,
  Such a little thing as I!

OH, what a service can I do,
  To repay her for her care?
For I can not even sew,
  Nor make any thing I wear.

The Little Beggar Boy

THERE'S a poor beggar going by,
  I saw him looking in,
He's just about as big as I,
  Only so very thin.

HE has no shoes upon his feet,
  He is so very poor:
And hardly any thing to eat
  I pity him, I'm sure,

BUT I have got nice clothes, you know,
  And meat, and bread, and fire;
And dear mamma, that loves me so,
  And all that I desire.

HERE, little boy, come back again,
  And hold that ragged hat,
And I will put a penny in,
  There, buy some bread with that.

18 The Rose-Bud

A FLOWER IN THE JUVENILE GARLAND CONSISTING OF SHORT POEMS ADAPTED TO THE UNDERSTANDING OF YOUNG CHILDREN

London: Printed for Baldwin and Cradock, Paternoster Row, 1831, third edition

Pride Reproved

"TO-MORROW is our dancing-day,
Miss Splendid will be there;
Mamma, do lend me something gay,
As ornaments, to wear.

"SHE has a watch, a locket, rings,
A necklace, bracelets too;
Besides a hundred other things,
Most beautiful to view."

"MY dear," her mother said, and smiled,
"Miss Splendid may do so;
I think she is an only child,
And I have six, you know.

"PERHAPS you wish I had them not,
But that the rest had died,
That you with what your friend has got,
May gratify your pride."

"NO, Mother, no," she said, with tears,
"I could not bear to part
With all the pretty little dears;
I love them from my heart.

"I SEE, dear Mother, I've been wrong;
You know what's best for me;
And, from this day, I'll never long
For any thing I see."

Sad Effects of Gunpowder

"I HAVE got a sad story to tell,"
Said Betty one day to Mamma:
"T'will be long, Ma'am, before John is well,
On his eye is so dreadful a scar.

"MASTER Wilful enticed him away,
To join with some more little boys;
They went in the garden to play,
And I soon heard a terrible noise.

"MASTER Wilful had laid a long train
Of Gunpowder, Ma'am, on the wall;
It has put them to infinite pain,
For it blew up, and injured them all.

"JOHN'S eyebrow is totally bare;
Tom's nose is bent out of its place;
Sam Bushy has lost all his hair,
And Dick White is quite black in the face."

The Affectionate Brother

LITTLE James, full of play,
Went shooting one day,
Not thinking his Sister was nigh;
The arrow was low,
But the wind raised it so,
That it hit her just over the eye.

THIS good little lad
Was exceedingly sad
At the sorrow he caused to his sister;
He looked at her eye,
And said, "Emma, don't cry;"
And then, too, he tenderly kiss'd her.

SHE could not then speak;
And it cost her a week
Before she recover'd her sight;
And James burn'd his bow
And his arrows, and so
I think little James acted right.

19 The Pink

A FLOWER IN THE JUVENILE GARLAND, CONSISTING OF SHORT POEMS, ADAPTED TO THE UNDERSTANDING OF YOUNG CHILDREN

London: Printed for Baldwin and Cradock, Paternoster Row, 1834, third edition

Good Little Fred

WHEN Little Fred
Was call'd to bed,
He always acted right;

HE kiss'd Mamma,
And then Papa,
And wish'd them both good night.

HE made no noise,
Like naughty boys,
But quietly up stairs

DIRECTLY went,
When he was sent,
And always said his prayers.

Short Advice

HEAR
Dear
Little son;
Go
Slow,
Do not run.

NEAR
Here
Is a well;
Poor
Moore
In it fell.

DOWN
Town
Do not stray;
There
Dare
Not to play.

DO
You
Make a rule;
Come
Home
Straight from school.

The Umbrella

ONCE as little Isabella
Ventured, with a large Umbrella,
Out upon a rainy day,
She was nearly blown away.

LUCKILY her good Mamma
Saw her trouble from afar;
Running just in time, she caught her
Pretty little flying daughter.

Give with Prudence

"I SEE, Mamma," said little Jane,
A beggar coming down the lane;
O, let me take him (may not I?)
This cheesecake and some currant pie."

"YOUR charity I much approve,
And something you may take him, love;
But let it be some bread and cheese,
Much better than such things as these.

"BY giving sweetmeats to the poor,
Who never tasted them before,
We spoil the good we have in view,
And teach them wants they never knew."

Grateful Lucy

AS LUCY with her mother walk'd,
She play'd and gambol'd, laugh'd and talk'd,
Till, coming to the river side,
She slipp'd, and floated down the tide.

HER faithful Carlo being near,
Jump'd in to save his mistress dear;
He drew her carefully to shore,
And Lucy lives and laughs once more.

"DEAR gen'rous Carlo," Lucy said,
"You ne'er shall want for meat and bread;
For every day before I dine
Good Carlo shall have some of mine."

Thoughtless Julia

JULIA did in the window stand;
Mamma, then sitting by,
Saw her put out her little hand
And try to catch a fly.

"O DO NOT hurt the pretty thing;"
Her prudent Mother said;
"Crush not its leg or feeble wing,
So beautifully made.

"IN Papa's book, 'Take not away
The life you cannot give,
For all things have (you'll read one day)
An equal right to live."

Hot Apple Pie

AS CHARLES his sisters sat between,
An Apple Pie was brought;
Slily to get a piece unseen,
The little fellow thought.

A PIECE from off Sophia's plate
Into his mouth he flung;
But, ah! repentance came too late,
It burn'd his little tongue.

Put Down the Baby

"O DEAR MAMMA," said little Fred,
"Put baby down—take me instead;
Upon the carpet let her be,
Put baby down, and take up me."

"NO, that, my dear, I cannot do,
You know I used to carry you;
But you are now grown strong and stout,
And you can run, and play about."

Stingy Peter

PETER CAREFUL had a cake,
Which his kind Mamma did bake;
Of butter, eggs, and currants made,
And sent it to him—*carriage paid.*

HE, like Harry (sad to say)
Did not give a bit away,
But, miser-like, the cake he locks,
With all his playthings, in his box.

WHEN next he went (it makes me laugh)
He found the mice had eaten half;
And what remain'd, tho' once a treat,
So mouldy, 'twas not fit to eat.

The Snow Ball

LITTLE Edward lov'd to go
Playing in the drifted snow,
Like some little boys I know;
COLD EDWARD!

HE a solid Snow ball made,
(Friendly tricks at home he play'd)
Which he in his pocket laid;
WISE EDWARD!

VERY hard that day it freez'd
Very hard the ball was squeez'd,
And he trotted home well pleas'd;
SLY EDWARD!

BY the fire he took a seat,
Thoughtless of the pow'r of heat;
Drops fall trickling on his feet;
WET EDWARD!

NOW the snow began to melt,
Vainly on the ground he knelt,
All now laugh'd at what he felt;
POOR EDWARD!

20 Simple Stories for Little Folk

BY TIMOTHY GOODWISE, SECOND EDITION IMPROVED

Portland: S. H. Colesworthy, 1836

The Gentleman

THE gentleman is a man who has but little to do—who lives upon the interest of his money, and walks about the street. I would rather be an industrious mechanic.

The Drunkard

O, HOW I should hate to be a drunkard! Tom Watkins was once a sober man; he loved his wife and children, and provided well for his family. Now he gets drunk every day. See him quarreling at the retailer's door. He don't care who sees him now, and

he swears very badly. He has now gone home to vex and torment his sick wife and destitute children. How sorry I should be to have my father drink rum and get drunk. I think it would not make me feel so bad to go up in the grave yard and read his name upon a tomb stone. I declare I'll never get drunk. I'll die first.

Old Dick

OLD DICK was a real toper. From morn to noon, from noon to night he was a companion of the bottle. Once the stage left him, because he stopped too long to take his bitters, and Old Dick bawled lustily for the driver to stop, but he would n't hear to him. He did just right.

My Cousin

HA! HA! how glad I am to see cousin Cadavarous. Oh, how tidy he looks!

O, HOW delighted aunt Sukey is at the Concert!

Land and Water Boat

NOW HERE'S a boat that's worth looking at. She'll run on the land and sea too. O, how I should like to sail in her. How complete we'd go.

MARM, our Hannah is going to school without milking the cow. Shan't I call her back, marm. She's running like old Sancho, to get away.

GOOD lady, will you give me some plums? I am a poor boy and mother has to make soap for a living. My father died many years ago, but he was a good man.

Ichabod

I AM surprised that Ichabod is so idle, when his parents are so good to him. He has come near losing his life once or twice. The other day he was stung by some bees. If he lives he will become, I dare not say what.

My Last Page

NOW children, I have come to my last page, and what shall I say? Be good boys and girls and be obedient to your parents and teachers, and you will be happy. When you get to be old you will be as contented and cheerful as Timothy Goodwise. See his house, how nicely it is finished. He has earned it by industry and perseverance. But as it is now getting late, and feeling quite tired, I now bid you good bye.

21 Select Rhymes for the Nursery

New-York: Mahlon Day, 374 Pearl-Street, 1836

Good Mamma

LOVE, come and sit upon my knee,
And give me kisses, one, two, three,
And tell me whether you love me,
MY BABY.

FOR this I'm sure, that I love you,
And many, many things I do,
And all day long I sit and sew
FOR BABY.

AND when you see me pale and thin,
By grieving for my baby's sin,
I think you'll wish that you had been
A BETTER BABY.

The Infant Baby

LOOK at his pretty shining hair;
His cheeks so red, his skin so fair;
His curly ringlets just like flax;
His little bosom just like wax!

I think he's growing very wise;
Now, don't you think so? Julia cries,
Then to the cradle off she ran,
To kiss the little fairy-man.

Getting Up

BABY, baby, ope your eye,
For the sun is in the sky,
And he's peeping once again
Through the frosty window pane;
Little baby, do not keep
Any longer fast asleep.

22 The Slave's Friend

FROM THE SLAVE'S FRIEND, VOLS. I & II

For Sale at the Anti-Slavery Office, Corner of Nassau and Spruce Sts., New York, 1836

Selling Slaves by the Pound

CHARLES. Did you ever know, Papa, that slaves were sold by the pound before Mr. Birney wrote that letter?

PAPA. Certainly I did. Did you never hear that before?

CHARLES. What, sell boys and girls, like Julia and me, as they do pigs and fish! Is it so, father? Tell us.

PAPA. It is indeed true, my son. If you will look into Mr. Bourne's book, PICTURE OF SLAVERY, you will see some slaves weighing a little girl in a pair of scales.

CHARLES. How much will she weigh?

PAPA. I suppose about fifty pounds.

CHARLES. How much do they get a pound for the poor slaves?

PAPA. Four dollars, and sometimes five: If that little girl weighed fifty pounds, and her master got four dollars a pound for her, she was sold for two hundred dollars.

CHARLES. Ah! That's the reason they dont want to emancipate the slaves; they get so much money by selling them: Isn't it so, father?

The Petition

Of the Sugar-making Slaves—humbly addressed to the consumers of sugar.

YOU no wish that we should suffer,
Gentle Massa, we are sure;
You quite willing we be happy,
If you see it in your power.

WE are very long kept toiling,
Fifteen hours in every day;
And the night for months is added,
Wearing all our strength away.

'TIS because you love our sugar,
And so *very much* you buy;
Therefore day and night we labor,
Labor, labor till we die.

O! IF less could e'er content you,
Or you'd buy from Eastern isles,
You would fill our hearts with gladness,
And our tearful eyes with smiles.

THEN we should have time to rest us,
And our weary eyes might sleep;
We could raise provision plenty,
And we might the Sabbath keep.

'TWOULD not hurt us, Massa gentle,
If you should our sugar leave;
We should only fare the better,
So for us you need not grieve.

'TIS while plenty sugar's wanted,
That we suffer more and more:
Ease us, Massa, ease our sorrow!
See, it is within your power.

IT should be enough for Massa,
If we work as English do;
All to want poor Negro's sugar,
Makes our toil a killing wo.

Illustrations in this column are from "Tom Steady, A Pretty History for Good Children," published by the American Tract Society, No. 150 Nassau Street, New York, circa 1840.

23 Fanny Overkind

J. Wrigley, Publisher, 61 Chatham Street, N. Y.

FANNY OVERKIND.

Fanny Giving a Poor Boy Plum Cake.

Fanny Overkind, was too kind by half; she thought she could not do enough although being stingy, is a bad thing of any one, still being a good natured fool is I think much worse.

Fanny one day met a poor little boy coming into the house with a basket and asking for cold victuals; instead

Fanny Watering her Little Garden.

of giving him that, she went to the store room and brought him down a large peice of rich plumb cake, which he eat all up; and made himself very sick for he was not used to such rich food. Then Fanny had a little garden of her own, that she took great care of at least; she thought she did, but

Little Fanny and her Young Ducks.

the fact is she took too much care of it: sometimes the little birds, and chickens, would be picking at the plants, so Fanny had a nett made to cover her flowers and keep the chickens away; but if she had not put the nett over her garden the plants would not have died as they

Fanny Frighted at the Mice.

did: for the chickens, and birds, were only picking off the caterpillar and bugs: that would eat the young plants. But Fanny, did not know that: again sometimes when it would be raining. Fanny would go out with a large umbrella, and try to keep it over a brood of young

Little Fanny Leading the Horse Along.

ducks so that they would not get wet; when she ought to know that they liked to have the rain come down on them; for you know, it is their nature to be in the water, sometimes, Fanny thought it very cruel to set traps to catch the poor little mice, as she would call them; so she

Fanny Leting the Bird out of its Cage.

would not have any mouse traps about the house; and now she can never sit down to her dinner: but she has all the mice in the house to help her to eat it. But I must tell you; the funniest thing she done, one day seeing a very old horse drawing a market cart along the road; and an

The Funeral of Fanny's Dickey Bird.

old woman driveing it Fanny thought she would help the poor old horse, so what does she do, but try to pull it along by the rains ! when the horse took and eat up her new straw hat right off her head. Fanny thought it too cruel to keep her little canary bird, Dickey shut up in the cage, all the time, so she let it out, and the next minute the cat killed him for he was too young to fly far; and had lighted on the ground where the cat caught him. Fanny had a funeral for him and had Dickey bured, in the garden under a rose bush.

II/ *Nursery Rhymes*

THE FIRST serious effort to collect, trace and classify the nursery rhymes of England was made by J. O. Halliwell-Phillipps in 1841. Andrew Lang, who later edited a collection for popular use, leaned heavily on Halliwell's work, as did Iona and Peter Opie, who in recent years reclassified this material with additions of their own. The various claims made for the origins of specific rhymes are often speculative. But a strong probability emerges that most popular nursery rhymes are remaining fragments of adult oral lore.

Johan Huizinga (*Homo Ludens*), in tracing the origins of play, states that "culture is first played in the form of a game." But it is also true that cultural fragments on the decline again become playthings when they are no longer taken seriously. The ballad that is no longer topical, the obsolete street cry of the hawker, are examples of some of the material that makes up the culture of the nursery. Even among the children themselves there is a descent of games, play and interests that seep from the older age groups to the younger. The fad of today's teen-ager ends up as the toy of tomorrow's pre-school child.

Nursery rhymes serve a twofold purpose. They are soporifics, and they are speech play. They are spoken or sung to babies almost entirely by adults or teen-age baby sitters at a time when the baby's speech consists of coos, gurgles and cries, while his comprehension is limited to inflection and tone rather than to content. Nursery rhymes don't have to make sense, and if they happen to do so, it is probably accidental. It is more than likely that adults used portions of popular ballads that they happened to recall while rocking baby to sleep or fondling him. Therefore nursery rhymes, as opposed to children's game rhymes, are probably predominantly fragments of adult lore, quite meaningless when seen out of their original context.

As shown in the following pages, only the first stanza of "Little Tommy Tucker" and segments of "Simple Simon" and "Little Jack Horner" have survived. These, among others, descended from adult oral tradition to the lower-class adult chapbook and ended eventually in the nursery. Many other surviving nursery rhymes may have had a similar history, their original sources having disappeared in the intervening centuries. As such nursery rhymes came to depend on print for transmission it was inevitable that each succeeding edition was based on those immediately preceding, instead of on original sources. Every edition was sifted and pruned so that the number of such rhymes kept shrinking. Here and there a rhyme crops up that was probably remembered by an author from his own childhood and that cannot be found elsewhere. Such isolated rhymes appear in early chapbooks for children, in folklore collections and even in the little advertising pamphlets given to children by manufacturers in the nineteenth century.

1 The Pleasant History of Jack Horner

CONTAINING HIS WITTY TRICKS AND PLEASANT PRANKS, WHICH HE PLAY'D FROM HIS YOUTH TO HIS RIPER YEARS: RIGHT PLEASANT AND DELIGHTFUL FOR WINTER AND SUMMER RECREATIONS

Newcastle: Printed in This Present Year (no date)

JACK HORNER was a pretty lad,
Near London he did dwell,
His father's heart he made full glad
His mother lov'd him well;
She often set him on her lap,
To turn him dry beneath
And fed him with sweet sugar'd pap,
Because he had no teeth.
While little Jack was sweet and young,
If he by chance should cry,
His mother pretty sonnets sung,
With a Lulla ba by;
With such a dainty, curious tone,
As Jack sat on her knee,
So that e'er he could go alone,
He sung as well as she.
A pretty boy, of curious wit,
All people spoke his praise
And in the corner he would sit
In Christmas holy-days:
When friends they did together meet,
To pass away the time;
Why, little Jack, he sure would eat
His Christmas pye in rhime,
And said, Jack Horner, in the corner,
Eats good Christmas pye,
And with his thumbs pulls out the plumbs,
And said Good boy am I,
These pretty verses which he made
Upon his Christmas cheer,
Did gain him love, as it is said,
Of all both far and near.

[Jack Horner's tale went on to many adventures, some bawdy, others similar in manner to those of Tom Thumb, whom he resembled in stature as in style. However, he is eventually debased to a four-line stanza that survives only in child literature to be incorporated as a standard item in Mother Goose's collected rhymes. Similarly "The Three Wise Men Of Gotham" have their origin in the folktale chapbook. Authorship of the original tales of these madcap nonsense figures is attributed to one Andrew Boorde who, after a quite colorful life, expired in Fleet Jail in London in 1549.—A.A.]

FRONTISPIECE: *The Merry Tales of the Wise Men of Gotham.*

2 Simple Simon

FROM THE ROYAL BOOK OF NURSERY RHYMES

London: Published by Ryle and Paul, 2 & 3, Monmouth Court, Seven Dials (no date)

ONCE Simon made a great snow ball
  And brought it in to roast,
He laid it down before the fire,
  And soon the ball was lost.

SIMON was sent to market,
  To buy a joint of meat,
He tied it to his horse's tail,
  To keep it clean and sweet.

HE went for water in a sieve,
  But soon it all run through,
And went all o'er his clothes,
  Which made poor Simon rue.

Simple Simon illustrations in "The Royal Book of Nursery Rhymes."

3 Nurse Love-Child's Legacy

London: Printed by J. Catnach, 2 Monmouth Court, Seven Dials (no date)

Nurse Love-Child's

L EGACY

LONDON:

Printed by J. Catnach, 2, Monmouth Court, 7 Dials.

WHAT is the news of the day,
Good neighbour I pray,
They say the balloon,
Is gone up to the moon.

THE little mouse
Doth skip and play,
He runs by night,
And sleeps by day.

THIS is the Cat
That killed the Cock,
For waking her
At five o'clock.

WHO comes here
A Grenadier,
What do you want
A pot of beer,
Where's your money
I've forgot.
Get you gone
You drunken sot.

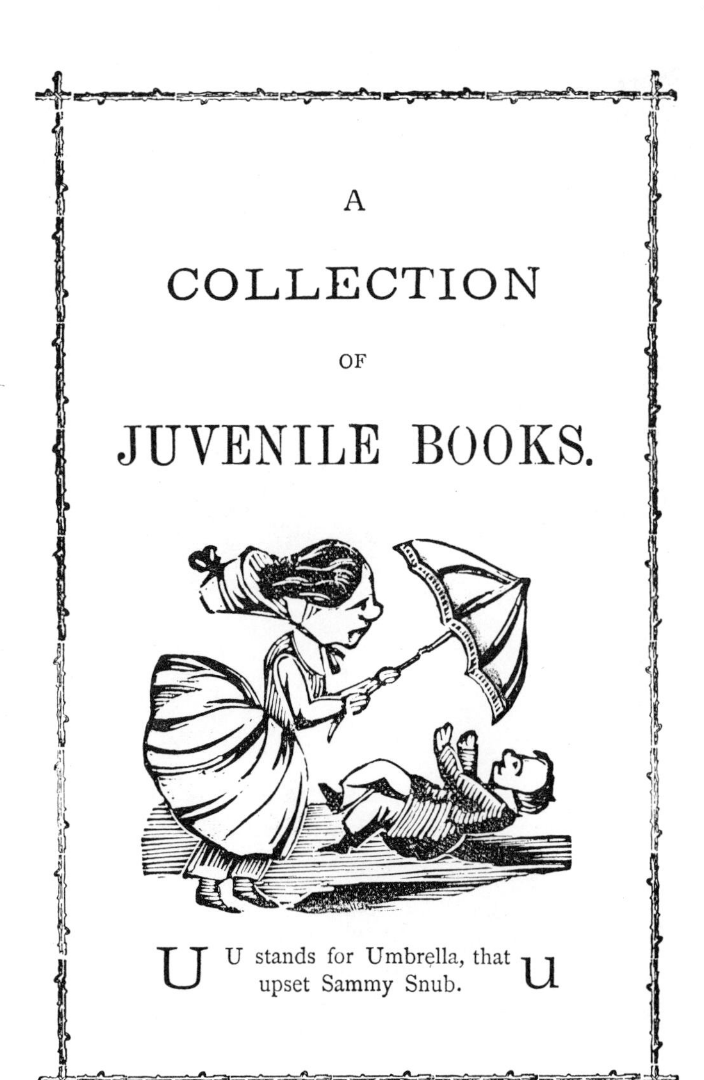

A

COLLECTION

OF

JUVENILE BOOKS.

U U stands for Umbrella, that upset Sammy Snub. U

V V is a Vessel made of a tub. V

X X is Xenophon, so famous in Story. X

Material on this page is from "A Collection of Juvenile Books Printed and Published by James Catnach."

4 The History of Little Tom Tucker

THIS IS LITTLE TOM TUCKER, THAT SUNG FOR HIS SUPPER

York: J. Kendrew, Printer, Colliergate, circa 1810

LITTLE Tom Tucker,
Sing for your supper,
What shall I sing for?
White bread and butter.
How shall I cut it,
Without a knife;
And how shall I marry
Without ever a wife?

THO' little Tom Tucker,
Loved white bread and butter,
He did not love learning
his book;
So when he went to school,
They drest him like a fool,
With a cap on his head,
only look.

TOM loved playing at top,
And often would stop
For to have a game in the street,
Tho' he knew 'twas a fault,
And if he was caught,
He well might expect to be beat.

HE loved for to play
By night or by day,
He could trundle the hoop
very well,
But though he knew better,
Than to learn one letter,
For fear they should
learn him to spell.

A MAN from the fair,
Came by with a bear,
With a monkey that rode
upon bruin;
Tom followed to see,
More blocked was he.
For it caus'd him to play
the truant.
At home he got blame,
When next morning came,
To school he went
creeping quite sad.

WHERE his master did flog,
And chain him to a log.
For being so naughty a lad,
Says Tom, this won't do,
I'm a dunce it is true,
All boys who can read are
my betters;
So he learnt A, B, C,
And D, E, F, G,
And soon all the rest of
his letters.

THEN Tom learned to spell,
And went to school well,
With satchel and books at
his back;
No more would he stay
To play by the way,
With Ned, Bill, Harry, or Jack.

TOM kept learning his book,
And cheerful did look,
Of the fool's cap no longer
in fear;
Got his master's good word,
Was head scholar preferr'd,
And the above fine medal
to wear.

ONE day he went out
And walking about,
He met an old woman quite
poor,
He gave her all his pence,
She returned him her thanks,
And hoped he would soon have
more.

ONE sun shining day,
He met a lady gay,
And he being grown a smart
youth,
He asked her to marry,
Not long did she tarry,
For Tom promis'd he'd love her
with truth.

NOW Tom's got a wife,
And Tom's got a knife,
And Tom can sit down to
his supper,
As blest as a king,
And each night can sing,
After eating his white
bread and butter.

5 The Story of Little Sarah and Her Johnny-Cake

Boston: W. J. Reynolds & Co., circa 1830

LITTLE Sarah she stood by her grandmother's bed,
"And what shall I get for your breakfast?" she
said;
"You shall get me a Johnny-cake: quickly go
make it,
In one minute mix, and in two minutes bake it."

So Sarah she went to the closet to see
If yet any meal in the barrel might be.
The barrel had long time been empty as wind;
Not a speck of the bright yellow meal could she
find.

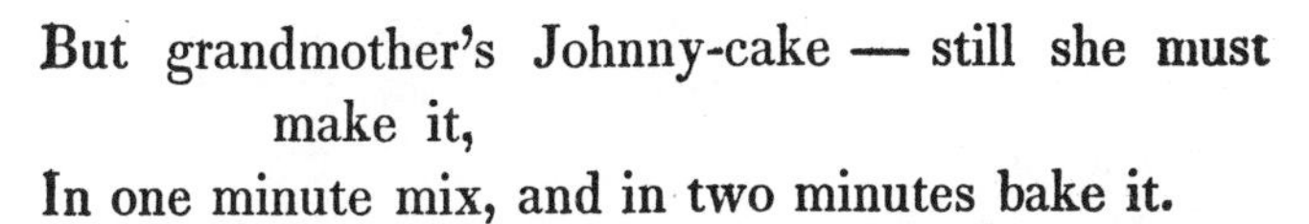

But grandmother's Johnny-cake — still she must
make it,
In one minute mix, and in two minutes bake it.

She ran to the shop; but the shopkeeper said,
" I have none — you must go to the miller, fair
maid;
" For he has a mill, and he'll put the corn in it,
And grind you some nice yellow meal in a minute;

But run, or the Johnny-cake, how will you
make it,
In one minute mix, and in two minutes bake it?"

Then Sarah she ran every step of the way;
But the miller said, " No, I have no meal to-day;
Run, quick, to the cornfield, just over the hill,
And if any be there, you may fetch it to mill.

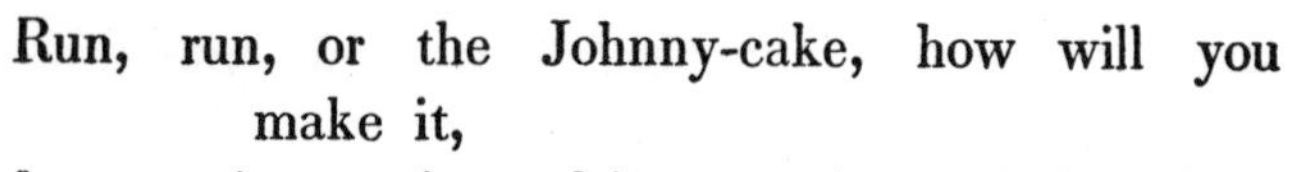

Run, run, or the Johnny-cake, how will you
make it,
In one minute mix, and in two minutes bake it?"

She ran to the cornfield — the corn had not grown,
Though the sun in the blue sky all pleasantly shone.
"Pretty sun," cried the maiden, "please make the
corn grow."
"Pretty maid," the sun answered, "I cannot do
so."

"Then grandmother's Johnny-cake — how shall I
make it,
In one minute mix, and in two minutes bake it?"

Then Sarah looked round, and she saw what was
wanted;
The corn could not grow, for no corn had been
planted.

She asked of the farmer to sow her some grain,
But the farmer he laughed till his sides ached again.
"Ho! ho! for the Johnny-cake — how can you make it,
In one minute mix, and in two minutes bake it?"

The farmer he laughed, and he laughed out aloud, —
"And how can I plant till the earth has been ploughed?

Run, run to the ploughman, and bring him with speed;
He'll plough up the ground, and I'll fill it with seed."

Away, then, ran Sarah, still hoping to make it,
In one minute mix, and in two minutes bake it.

The ploughman he ploughed, and the grain it was
sown,
And the sun shed his rays till the corn was all
grown;
It was ground at the mill, and again in her bed
These words to poor Sarah the grandmother said:
"You shall get me a Johnny-cake — quickly go
make it,
In one minute mix, and in two minutes bake it."

6 Mother Goose's Melodies

SELECTED AND ARRANGED BY MY UNCLE SOLOMON

DEAR children, I have come again.
This is my closing story;
For I am old and full of pain
And overrun with glory.

BUT you will find this little book
Is full of everything.

LITTLE king Boggen, he built a fine hall,
Pie-crust and pastry-crust, that was the wall;
The windows were made of black-puddings and white,
And slated with pancakes—you ne'er saw the like.

THE man in the wilderness asked me,
How many strawberries grew in the sea?
I answered him as I thought good,
As many red herrings as grew in the wood,
And I would tell him if I could.

LAVENDER blue, and Rosemary green,
When I am king, you shall be queen;
Call up my maids at four of the clock,
Some to the wheel, and some to the rock;
Some to make cake, and some to shell corn,
And you and I will keep the bed warm.

WHEN I was a little boy, my father kept me in,
But now I am a great boy, fit to serve the king.
I can handle a musket, I can smoke a pipe,
I can kiss a pretty girl, at ten o'clock at night.

I HAD a little doll, the prettiest ever seen,
She washed me the dishes, and kept the house clean.

TRIP upon trenchers,
And dance upon dishes,
My mother sent me for yeast, some yeast,
She bid me tread lightly,
And come again quickly,
For fear some one would play me a jest.

GREAT A little a, bouncing B
The cat's in the cupboard, and she can't see.

LITTLE Jack a dandy,
Loved plum cake and sugar candy,
He bought some at a grocer's shop,
And out he comes, hop, hop, hop.

1. Let us go to the wood, says this pig;
2. What to do there? says that pig;
3. To look for my mother, says this pig;
4. What to do with her? says that pig;
5. To kiss her to death, says this pig.

WHAT care I how black I be,
Twenty pounds will marry me,
If twenty won't, why forty shall
For I am mamma's darling gal.

LAZY Tom with his jacket blue,
Stole his father's gouty shoe.
The worst of harm that dad can wish him,
Is his gouty shoe may fit him.

A BOAT, a boat, to cross the ferry,
For we are going to be merry.

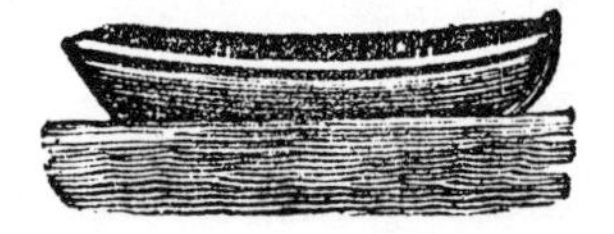

DINGTY, diddledy, my mama's maid,
She stole oranges, I am afraid;
Some in her pockets, some in her sleeves,
She stole oranges, I do believe.

FOUR and twenty tailors went to kill a snail,
The best man among them dare not touch her tail,
She put out her horns like a little kyloe cow,
Run, tailors, run, or she'll kill you all e'en now.

THE sow came in with a saddle,
The little pig rock'd the cradle,
The dish jump'd a top on the table,
To see the pot wash the ladle;
The spit that stood behind a bench,
Call'd the dishclout dirty wench;

ODDS plut, says the gridiron,
Can't ye agree,
I'm the head constable,
Bring 'em to me.

SATURDAY night shall be my whole care,
To powder my locks and curl my hair;
On Sunday morning my love will come in,
And marry me then with a pretty gold ring.

AS I was going to sell my eggs,
I met a thief with bandy legs,
Bandy legs and crooked toes,
I tript his heels and he fell on his nose.

I WON'T be my father's Jack,
I won't be my father's Jill,
I will be the fiddler's wife,
And have music when I will.
T'other little tune, t'other little tune,
Prythee, love, play me t'other little tune.

THE little dog turned round the wheel,
And set the bull a roaring,
And drove the monkey in the boat,
Who set the oars a rowing.
And scared the cock upon the rock,
Who cracked his throat with crowing.

WHEN I was a little boy, I lived by myself,
And all the bread and cheese I got,
I laid upon the shelf;
The rats and the mice, they made such a strife,
That I was forced to go to town,
And buy me a wife.

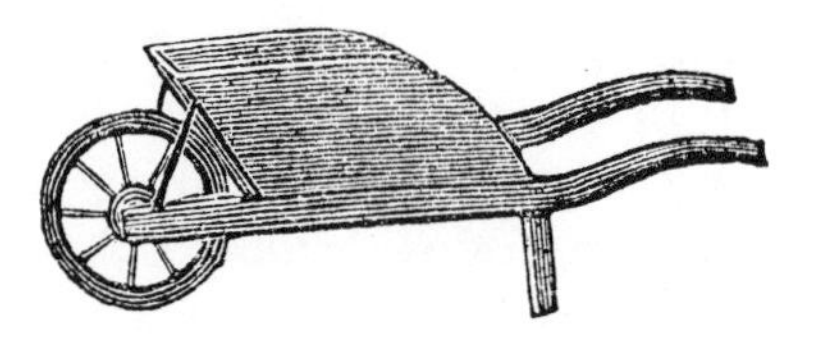

THE street was so broad, the lanes were so narrow,
I was forced to bring my wife home,
In a wheelbarrow;
The wheelbarrow broke, and my wife had a fall,
Farewell wife, wheelbarrow and all.

III/ *Street Cries*

THE street crier announcing his wares, fuel, fish or vegetables to sell, rags to buy, old shoes to mend, or knives to grind, penetrated the public consciousness as much in the centuries preceding as do radio and television commercials of today. The claim to "taste good like a cigarette should" is however much less poetic than its progenitors. Though this message may insinuate itself indelibly into the unconscious of today's television viewers, it is not likely that this or any other contemporary commercial catch phrase will become a part of traditional folklore, as did the commercials of an earlier age.

The street cries of London and Paris up to the beginning of the nineteenth century were the subject of many penny sheets and children's chapbooks. It is not to be assumed that these were the actual street cries used, though they are based on those that were commonly heard.

> Addison accuses the London street criers of cultivating the accomplishment of crying their wares so as not to be understood; . . . J. T. Smith says that the no longer heard cry of "Holloway Cheese Cakes" was pronounced "All my teeth ache;" . . . while . . . an old man who dealt in brick-dust, used to shout something that sounded exactly like "Do you want a lick on the head?"*

* Andrew W. Tuer, *Old London Street Cries*, 1885.

1 The Cries of London

London: Printed by J. Catnach, 2 Monmouth Court, Seven Dials (no date)

Cherries

HERE'S round and sound,
Black and white heart cherries,
Two-pence a pound.

Oranges

HERE'S oranges nice!
At a very small price,
I sell them all two for a penny.
Ripe, juicy, and sweet,
Just fit for to eat,
So customers buy a good many.

Toys

HERE'S your toys, for
girls and boys,
Only a penny, or a dirty
phial or bottle.

Milk Below

RAIN, frost, or snow, or
hot or cold,
I travel up and down,
The cream and milk you buy
of me
Is best in all the town.
For custards, puddings, or for tea,
There's none like those you buy of me.

Crumpling Codlings

COME, buy my Crumpling
Codlings,
Buy all my Crumplings.
Some of them you may eat
raw,
Of the rest make dumplings,
Or pies, or puddings, which
you please.

Filberts

COME, buy my filberts
ripe and brown,
They are the best in all the
town,
I sell them for a groat a
pound,
And warrant them all good and sound,
You're welcome for to crack and try,
They are so good I'm sure you'll buy.

2 American Street Cries

FROM JUVENILE PASTIMES, IN VERSE

Publisher unknown, circa 1820

New Milk

Radishes!

Sweep O!

Matches!

Strawberries!

Scissors to Grind!

Hot Corn!

Potatoes, O!

Clams! Clams!

Locks or Keys

IV/ *Fairy Tales*

MYTHS and tales of antiquity often explained what seemed inexplicable, marvelous and mysterious. They consisted of the exploits of heroes and villains made legendary. Often the deeds of whole groups of kings, nobles and wrongdoers were lumped together and attributed to a single symbolic individual whose stature grew to gigantic proportions.

The European legends of pre-Christian times, undercurrents of the Dark and Middle Ages, might well have become the basis for a new religion had not the established Church held such sway as to be able to relegate some to superstitious heresy and taken others unto itself. But even this could not eliminate the pagan tales entirely. They were perpetuated in the castle and at the peasant's hearth.

New material was grafted onto the old, embellished from Greek and Roman sources. Returning Crusaders added to this lore from Arabian tales and the Indian fables of Pilpay. Troubadours and minnesingers gathered and enlarged and spread them across all of Europe. They were taken as seriously and as literally as had been Homer's tales of Odysseus.

By the time some of the stories were set in print they were already cloaked in half-humorous disbelief. Yet who could be sure that hobgoblins and giants did not indeed lurk off the beaten forest path, made eerie by nocturnal howls of wolves that still roamed Europe at the beginning of the nineteenth century?

As the countryside became populous, as people traveled, were made more familiar with nature, and learned to be unafraid, the tales of ogres, dragons, witches and dwarfs became the stuff with which to frighten and amuse babies. The stories became and remain the exclusive property of children.

It would be futile to reprint here the stories gathered by Perrault, the indefatigable brothers Grimm, and Andersen. All are still in print and in popular usage, annotated and compared by anthropologists and folklorists, re-edited in countless editions. They retain their delightful flavor that can never be lost even in the retelling. Of interest to the reader should be some typical renditions that have come down almost intact from adult chapbooks, and that are reproduced on the following pages.

1 The Children in the Wood

THE MOST LAMENTABLE AND DEPLORABLE HISTORY OF THE TWO CHILDREN IN THE WOOD

Containing the happy Loves and Lives of their Parents, the Treachery and barbarous Villany of their Unkle, the duel between the Murdering Ruffians, and the unhappy and deplorable death of the two innocent Children.

As also an Account of the Justice of God that overtook the Unnatural Unkle; and of the deserved Death of the two murdering Ruffians.

HERE is a classic example of the folk ballad of the eighteenth century, appearing first in printed form about 1700, and eventually finding its way into children's literature in the late eighteenth and early nineteenth centuries. Reproduced in facsimile is Dunigan's edition, published in New York circa 1825.

SHRUBLAND HALL.

Deep seated in a flowery vale,

Beside a woody dell,

Stood Shrubland Hall, where, says the tale,

A worthy pair did dwell.

THE CHILDREN WITH THEIR PARENTS

Two beauteous babes this happy pair,

To crown their loves had got:

The proudest monarch on his throne,

Might envy them their lot.

THE UNCLE TAKING THE CHILDREN.

But death, in midst of all their joys,

Did seize this loving pair,

Who, dying, left their girl and boy

Unto an Uncle's care.

THE UNCLE BRIBING THE RUFFIANS

But to their fortunes he aspired,

And to secure his prey,

He two unfeeling Ruffians hired

To take their lives away.

THE RUFFIANS WITH THE CHILDREN.

These wretches, cruel, fierce and bold,

Conveyed them to a wood,

There, for the sake of filthy gold,

To shed their infant blood.

THE RUFFIANS FIGHTING.

But one his purpose did repent,

Before the deed was done,

And slew the other Ruffian there,

Then left the babes alone.

THE CHILDREN IN THE WOOD.

Their little hearts with terror sank,

With hunger, too, they cried,

At length upon a flowery bank

They laid them down, and died.

THE CHILDREN'S DEATH.

The Redbreasts, in their clustering bowers,

Sung mournful on each spray,

And there with leaves and fragrant flowers,

O ersprea d them as they lay.

All illustrations on this page are from "The History of Sir Richard Whittington," published about 1770.

2 Adventures of Little Red Riding Hood

MARKS' EDITION

Published by Fisk & Little, 82 State-Street, Albany, New York, circa 1820

In a little Thatched Cot, by the side of a Wood,
Lived an innocent lass, Little Red Riding Hood;
You would scarce find her equal, the neighbours all say,
So kind and obedient, so cheerful and gay.

One day this young lass,
To her Grandma was sent,
A nice pot of Butter,
To her to present;
Besides a Cheesecake,
And a new loaf of Bread,
For Grandma was ill,
And confined to her Bed.

But her Mother before
She set out on her way,
Charged her not on her journey
To loiter or play;
This charge she neglected,
And rambled for hours,
To gather Primroses,
And other wild flowers.

So she wandered about
Till the close of the day,
When the wicked old Wolf,
He came prowling that way,
He enquired her errand,
She soon let him know
Ah! silly young creature,
Why did you do so?

Away ran the Wolf,
While his heart did rejoice,
And he knocked at the door,
And spoke in a feign'd voice;
The Old Dame who for
Her Grand-daughter did watch
Cried pull up the bobbin,
Twill open the latch.

So he open'd the door,
And run up stairs with speed.
Poor Grandmamma was
Very much frightened indeed;
But he tore her to pieces,
Oh! merciless beast,
To make of a poor
Harmless Lady a Feast.

Then he put the poor Lady's
Nightcap on his head,
And cunningly slipped himself
Into the bed;
And when Riding Hood knocked
As she'd oft done before,
Says the Wolf, pull the Bobbin
'Twill open the door.

Then up stairs she went,
And was struck with surprise,
When she saw his sharp teeth,
And his great goggle eyes;
She would have cried out,
But at her he flew,
And tore her to pieces,
And ate her up too.

3 Jack the Giant Killer

FROM JACK THE GIANT KILLER, ILLUSTRATED WITH COLORED ENGRAVINGS

T. W. Strong, Publisher and Engraver, No. 98 Nassau-Street, New-York: W. G. Cottrell and Co., No. 64 Cornhill, Boston

IN THE reign of the famous King Arthur, there lived near the Land's End of England, in the County of Cornwall, a worthy farmer, who had an only son named Jack. Jack was a boy of a bold temper; he took pleasure in hearing or reading stories of wizards, conjurers, giants, and fairies.

In those days there lived on St. Michael's Mount a huge giant. He dwelt in a gloomy cavern on the very top of the mountain, and used to wade over to the main land in search of his prey. When he came near, the people left their houses; and after he had glutted his appetite upon their cattle, he would throw half a dozen oxen upon his back, and tie three times as many sheep and hogs round his waist, and so march back to his own abode. The Giant had done this for many years, and the coast of Cornwall was greatly hurt by his thefts, and Jack boldly resolved to destroy him.

Jack therefore took a horn, shovel, pick-axe, and a dark lantern; and swam to the mount. There he fell to work at once; and before morning he had dug a pit twenty two feet deep, and almost as many broad. He covered it at the top with sticks and straw, and strewed some of the earth over them, to make it look just like solid ground. He then put his horn to his mouth, and blew so loud and long, that the Giant awoke and came towards Jack, roaring like thunder. "You saucy villain, I will broil you for my breakfast."

He had hardly spoken these words, when he tumbled headlong into the pit.

"Oh, oh, Mr. Giant!" said Jack, "have you found your way so soon to the bottom?"

The Giant now tried to rise; but Jack struck him a blow on the crown of his head with his pick axe, which killed him.

Now when the justices of Cornwall heard of this valiant action, they sent for Jack, and declared that he should always be called Jack, the Giant-Killer, and they also gave him a sword and belt, upon which was written in letters of gold—

> This is the valiant Cornish man,
> Who slew the giant Cormoran.

Another strange thing happened to Jack. It so turned out that he was followed by a monstrous Giant, called Kill'em-All; and as he was trying to escape, and running with all his might, he met a man loaded with soft wax, who told him that he was pursued by another great Giant, called "Eat-'em-All." "Indeed," said Jack, "Then we will contrive to kill both."

The man with the wax was very much frightened, and said, "How Jack?" "Leave that to me," says Jack; and saying this he took up a handful of wax, and waited for the two giants.

Jack waited very steady, and aiming the great piece of wax at the Giant, Eat'em-All, struck him in the middle of the forehead; and just at this minute Kill'em-All came up from the other way, and Jack stepping on one side, the two giants met their heads together with such force, that the wax kept them fast, and Jack killed both of them.

The news of Jack's exploit soon spread, and another Giant, Old Blunderbore, vowed to have revenge on Jack.

This Giant kept an enchanted castle, in the midst of a lonely wood. Now as Jack was taking a journey to Wales, he passed through this wood; and being weary, he sat down to rest by the side of a pleasant fountain, and there fell into a deep sleep.

The Giant came to the fountain for water, and found Jack there; and as the lines on Jack's belt showed who he was, the Giant lifted him up, and carried him to his castle.

The Giant took him into a large room, where lay the hearts and limbs of persons that had been lately killed; and he told Jack, with a horrid grin, that men's hearts, eaten with pepper and vinegar, were his nicest food; and also that he thought he should make a dainty meal on his heart. When he had said this, he locked Jack up in that room, while he went to fetch another Giant who lived in the same wood, to enjoy a dinner off Jack's flesh.

While he was away, Jack heard dreadful shrieks, groans, and cries, from many parts of the castle; and soon after he heard a mournful voice repeat these lines—

> Haste, valiant stranger, haste away,
> Lest you become the Giant's prey.
> On his return he'll bring another,
> Still more savage than his brother.

Jack ran to the window, and saw the two Giants coming along, arm in arm. This window was right over the gates of the castle.

Now there were two strong cords in the room. Jack made a large noose with a slip knot at the end of both, and as the Giants were coming through the iron gates, he threw the ropes over their heads. He then made

the other ends fast to a beam in the ceiling, and pulled with all his might till he had almost strangled them. When he saw that they were both quite black in the face, and had no strength left, he drew his sword, and slid down the ropes; and killed the Giants. Jack next took a great bunch of keys from the pockets of Blunderbore, and went into the castle again. He made a search through all the rooms; and in them found three ladies tied up by the hair of their heads, and almost starved to death. They told him that their husbands had been killed by the Giants.

"Ladies," said Jack, "I have put an end to the monster and his wicked brother; and I give you this castle and all the riches it contains, to make you some amends for the dreadful pains you have felt." He then gave them the keys of the castle, and went further on his journey.

At length he lost his way; and when night came on, he was in a valley between two lofty mountains. He thought himself lucky at last in finding a large and handsome house. He went to it, and knocked at the gate; when to his surprise there came forth a Giant with two heads. He bade Jack welcome, and led him into a room where he could pass the night. Soon after this he heard the Giant walking backward and forward in the next room, saying,

> Though here you lodge with me this night,
> You shall not see the morning light;
> My club shall dash your brains out quite.

Then getting out of bed, Jack groped about the room, and found a billet of wood; he laid it in his place in the bed, and hid himself in a corner of the room. In the middle of the night the Giant came with his great club, and struck many heavy blows on the bed, and in the very place where Jack had laid the billet; and then went to his own room, thinking he had broken all Jack's bones.

Early in the morning Jack walked into the Giant's room. The Giant started when he saw him, and began to stammer out, "Pray, how did you sleep last night? Did you hear or see any thing in the dead of night?" "Nothing worth speaking of," said Jack, "a rat, I believe, gave me three or four flaps with its tail, but I soon went to sleep again." The Giant did not answer a word, but brought in two bowls of hasty-pudding for their breakfasts. Jack contrived to button a leathern bag inside his coat, and slipped the pudding into the bag, instead of his mouth.

When breakfast was over, he said to the Giant, "I will show you a trick; I could cut my head off one minute, and put it on sound the next." He then took a knife, ripped up the bag, and all the pudding fell on the floor.

"Odds splutter hur nails," cried the Giant, who was ashamed to be outdone by Jack, "hur can do that hurself." So he snatched up the knife, plunged it into his stomach, and in a moment dropped down dead. After this Jack went on his journey.

In passing through a dense forest, he saw a huge Giant sitting on the top of a tree. As Jack came near, the giant saw him, and says, "O, ho, my fine fellow! I've got you safe enough." "Have you!" thought Jack, as he saw two great sacks nearly half full of turpentine and pitch, which some woodmen had left when they run away from the giant.

So Jack directly began pulling on his gloves, and then pulling them off, and then putting them on again, all which the Giant watched closely from his seat on the tree.

As soon as Jack saw that the Giant was tired of watching, he got behind a large cork tree, and saw the giant come down, roaring as loud as he could,

> "Now Giant-killing Master Jack,
> I'll smash your bones, and break your back."

But the Giant stopped short, and seeing the two sacks half full of pitch, began to pull them on as Jack had done his gloves,—and after a great deal of trouble the Giant got them on his two great hands,—but the sun was shining so hot, the sacks stuck to his hands, and he could not pull them off again; and Jack went boldly up to him, and killed him.

The news of his last exploit happening to reach the ears of Gumdaclitch, the first-cousin of the Giant that Jack had killed last, he vowed revenge, and came armed with a huge bow and steel pointed arrows.

Jack, however, was prepared for him with a huge loadstone, and finding the place where Gumdaclitch laid down to rest, and planting his loadstone in a right manner, contrived to draw away every arrow the Giant had, even his sword, which was ten feet long. And getting together heaps of straw and faggots of wood, Jack surrounded the Giant with them, and set fire to them.

The giant woke up in a great rage, but it was of no use, and Jack having seen him well roasted, caused a deep ditch to be digged, into which they rolled the Giant, and he died,—but so strong was he, that it took eight days and seven nights before the breath went out of his body—and the ground that covered him smoked and heaved for many years afterwards. After this last exploit, all the country rejoiced.

Jack then passed on to Land's End, where he had heard of a Giant, who, with his wife, dwelt on the top of a high hill. Now this Giant had four arms, as well as six heads; and always carried a huge club in each hand.

Meantime the Giant and his wife had heard of Jack's approach, and had got ready a huge stone which he named after himself,—and with which he meant to crush Jack directly should he approach.

But when Jack arrived, the Giant was quarelling with his wife, and did not notice him, and Jack, watching his opportunity, drew his sword and killed him.

V/ *Anthropomorphism*

CHILDREN'S stories in which human traits, thoughts, action, and speech are attributed to animals are a favorite bugaboo of today's librarians, teachers and children's book editors. Let just a single creature, other than human, express himself in fancifully sentient human terms, and the hue and cry of "anthropomorphism" is raised, as though it were a dirty and subversive thing for an author to do in public.

It is doubtful whether Aesop, writing today, could get editorial approval for his fables. Kenneth Grahame's *The Wind in the Willows* also probably could not find an initial publisher now.

It is true that cuteness for its own sake, bad taste, poor writing and lack of imagination are often cloaked in anthropomorphism. But it also badly underestimates the wit and whimsy of children to assume that they might take "Mother Hubbard" or "The Notorious Glutton" as gospel. There is even a vast difference between the hilarious antics of Walt Disney's original "Mickey Mouse" and his later, inhumanly human "Donald Duck." It would therefore seem appropriate to appraise the "talking animal" on a qualitative basis, rather than banish it entirely from children's literature.

At a time when supposedly serious scientists are speculating about the speech and communications patterns of dolphins, it does seem absurd that any book that attributes whimsical logic to an animal should suffer categorical interdiction.

In the early days of children's literature, largely as a result of the popularity of *Aesop's Fables*, authors were not quite as inhibited or repressed as they are now. They wrote many amusing anthropomorphic tales and ditties that enjoyed wide popularity. Not all of these were good books. But many were better than much of the pseudo-scientific children's literature of today. Some even helped children to look at the world from unorthodox points of view and were probably more stimulating to their imagination than those dry little works that pretend to be able to turn them into miniature Darwins.

1 Old Mother Hubbard and Her Wonderful Dog

London: J. Catnach, Printer and Publisher, 2 Monmouth Court, Seven Dials, circa 1800

OLD MOTHER HUBBARD went to the cupboard
To get the poor dog a bone;
But when she came there the cupboard was bare,
And so the poor dog had none.

SHE went to the baker's to buy him some bread,
When she came back the dog was dead.
Ah! my poor dog, she cried, oh, what shall I do?
You were always my pride—none equal to you.

SHE went to the undertaker's to buy him a coffin,
When she came back, the dog was laughing.
Now how this can be quite puzzles my brain,
I am much pleased to see you alive once again.

SHE went to the barber's to buy him a wig,
When she came back he was dancing a jig.
O, you dear merry grig, how nicely you're prançing;
Then she held up the wig, and he began dancing.

TO market she went, to buy him some tripe,
When she came back he was smoking his pipe.
Why, sure, cried the dame, you'd beat the great Jocko,
Who before ever saw a dog smoking tobacco?

SHE went to the sempstress to buy him some linen,
When she came back the dog was spinning.
The reel, when 'twas done, was wove into a shirt,
Which served to protect him from weather and dirt.

SHE went to the alehouse to buy him some beer,
When she came back he sat on a chair.
Drink hearty, said dame, there's nothing to pay,
'Twill banish your sorrow and moisten your clay.

SHE went to the tailor's to buy him a coat,
When she came back he was riding the goat.
What, you comical elf, the good dame cried,
Who would have thought a dog would so ride?

SHE went to the shop to buy him some shoes,
When she came back he was reading the news.
Sure none would believe (she laughed as she spoke),
That a dog could be found to drink ale and smoke.

SHE went to the hatter's to buy him a hat,
When she came back he was feeding the cat.
The sight made her stare, as he did it so pat,
While puss sat on the chair, so she showed him the hat.

SHE went to the hosier's, to buy him some hose,
When she came back he was drest in his clothes.
How now? cries the dame, with a look of surprise,
To see you thus drest, I scarce credit my eyes.

SHE went to the fruiterer's to buy him some fruit,
When she came back he was playing the flute.
Oh, you musical dog, you surely can speak:
Come, sing me a song, then he set up a squeak.

THE dog he cut capers, and turned out his toes,
'Twill soon cure the vapours, he such attitude shows.
The dame made a curtsey, the dog made a bow,
The dame said, Your servant, the dog said Bow wow.

SHE went to the tavern for white wine and red,
When she came back he stood on his head.
This is odd, said the dame, for fun you seem bred,
One would almost believe you'd wine in your head.

Illustration from "The History of Reynard the Fox," London, 1780.

2 The Butterfly's Ball, and Grasshopper's Feast

London: J. Catnach, 2 Monmouth Court, Seven Dials (no date)

COME *take up your hats,*
And away let us haste,
To the Butterfly's Ball,
Or the Grasshopper's Feast.

THE trumpeter Gad-fly,
Has summon'd the crew,
And the revels are now,
Only waiting for you.

ON the smooth shaved grass,
By the side of a wood,
Beneath a broad oak,
Which for ages has stood.

SEE the children of earth,
And the tenants of air,
To an evening's amusement,
Together repair.

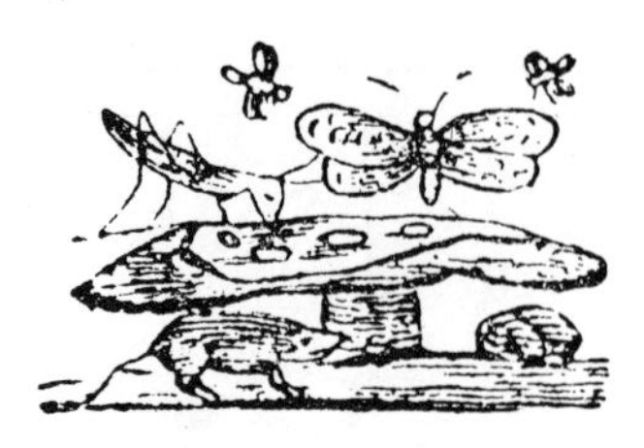

AND there came the Beetle,
So blind and so black,
And carried the Emmet,
His friend on his back.

AND there came the Gnat,
And the Dragon-fly too,
And all their relations—
Green, orange and blue.

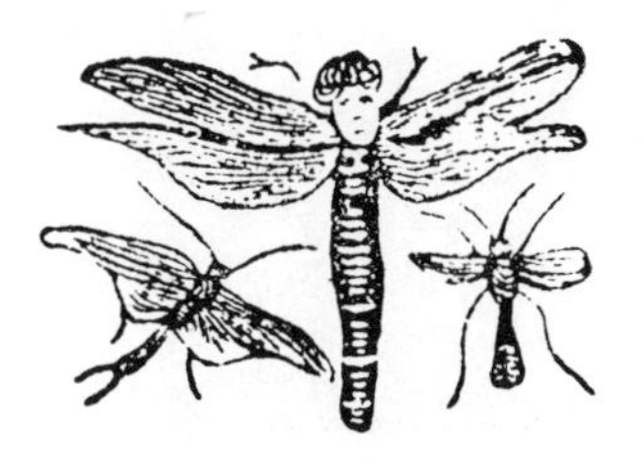

AND there came the Moth
With her plume of down,
And the Hornet with Jacket
Of yellow and brown.

WHO with him the Wasp,
His companion did bring,
But they promised that evening
To lay by their sting.

THE sly little Doormouse,
Peep'd out of his hole,
And lead to the feast,
His blind cousin the Mole.

AND the Snail with his horns,
Peeping out of a shell.
Came fatigued with the distance,
The length of an ell.

A Mushroom the table,
And on it was spread,
A water-dock leaf,
Which their table-cloth made.

THE viands were various,
To each of their taste,
And the Bee brought the honey,
To sweeten the feast.

WITH steps most majestic,
The Snail did advance,
And he promised the gazers
A minuet to dance.

BUT they all laugh'd so loud,
That he drew in his head,
And went in his own
Little chamber to bed.

THEN as the evening gave way
To the shadows of night,
Their watchman the glow-worm
Came out with his light.

SO home let us hasten,
While yet we can see,
For no watchman is waiting,
For you or for me.

THE

BUTTERFLY'S BALL

AND

Grasshopper's Feast.

TITLE-PAGE ILLUSTRATION: *The Butterfly's Ball*

3 Death and Burial of Cock Robin

London: Printed by A. Ryle & Paul, 2 *Monmouth Court, Seven Dials* (*no date*)

THE thread of death runs through much of early children's literature, and with good reason. The funeral cortege passed frequently down the street, halting at neighbor's houses, and sometimes at one's very own home. The life span was shorter, mothers died of child-bed fever, and the child mortality rate was very high. Children were taught very early out of necessity, rather than morbidity, that death was a part of life. They were probably better off than today's children to whom death is something that only happens to the bad guy on television.—A. A.

WHO kill'd Cock Robin?
I said the sparrow,
With my bow and arrow.
I kill'd Cock Robin.

WHO caught his blood?
I, said the fish,
With my little dish—
I caught his blood.

THIS is the fish
That held the dish.

WHO saw him die?
I, said the fly
With my little eye—
I saw him die.

THIS is the fly
That saw him die.

WHO made his shroud?
I, said the beetle,
With my little needle—
I made his shroud.

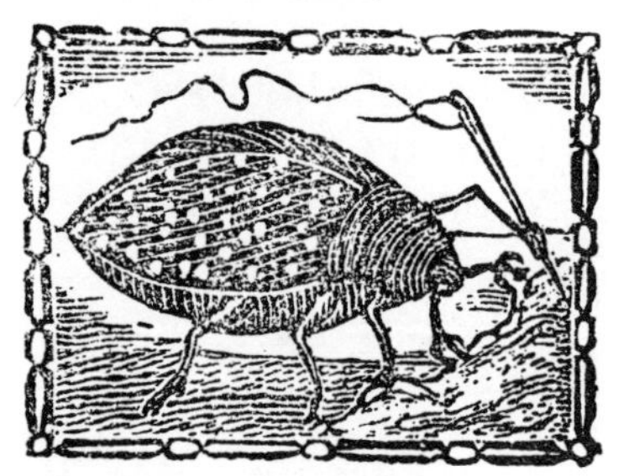

THIS is the beetle,
With his little needle.

WHO'LL be the parson?
I, said the rook,
With my little book—
I will be the Parson.

HERE is Parson Rook,
Reading his book.

WHO'LL carry the coffin?
I, said the Kite,
If it's not in the night—
I'll carry the coffin.

BEHOLD the Kite,
How he takes his flight.

WHO'LL be the clerk?
I, said the Lark,
If its not in the dark—
I will be the clerk.

BEHOLD how the Lark,
Says Amen like a clerk.

WHO will carry the link?
I, said the linnet:
I'll fetch it in a minute—
I will carry the link.

THE Linnet with a light,
Altho' it is not night.

4 Old Mother Mitten and Her Funny Kitten

FROM THE PRETTY PRIMER (THE JUVENILE GEM)

Huestis & Cozans, 104 Nassau Street, New York, circa 1825

OLD mother Mitten
And her pretty kitten,
Took supper, one night rather late;

BUT they sat down to tea,
And the dog came to see
Pussy cut the meat up on her plate.

THE dog and the cat
Were having a chat,
When Pussy cried out with a mew;

DEAR old mother Mitten,
Just look at your kitten,
She's going to drink mead with you.

WHEN the supper was over,
The kitten moreover,
Did stand on the top of her head.

SO the dog he declares,
They must sleep in their chairs,
And none of them get into bed.

SO when they awoke,
Miss Pussy first spoke,
And to the old Lady said she;

MY dear if you please,
Take this bread and cheese,
And I'll give you a hot cup of tea.

AT the table there sat,
The dog and the cat,
With cards they were trying to play;

BUT the dog's beard is long,
Which the cat thinks is wrong,
And here she is shaving poor Tray.

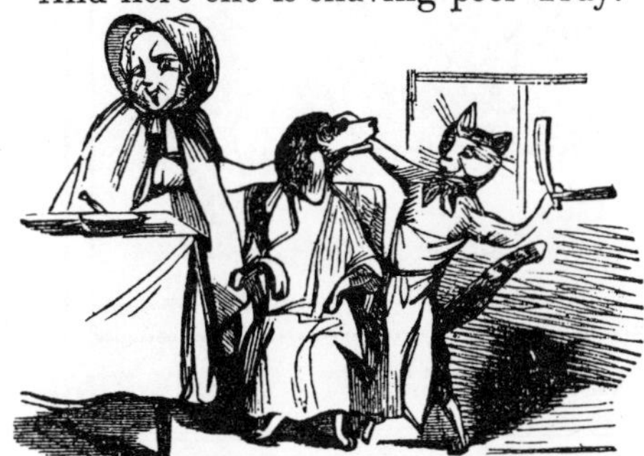

HAVING shaved Mr. Tray,
She hastens away,
And dresses herself for a walk;

AND when she came in,
Told where she had been,
To have with the neighbours a talk.

SAYS granny indeed,
I believe you're agreed,
To marry miss Puss, Mr. Tray;

THE dog made a bow,
And the cat she said mow,
And I think they got married that day.

5 Adventures of Puss in Boots

New York and Philadelphia: Turner and Fisher, no date

There once liv'd a young man, who was very poor,
  For all that he had was a Cat;
His food being gone, he could get no more,
  And so he resolved to kill that.
Now puss from the cupboard came out, and thus spoke,
  "Grieve not, my good master, I pray,
Provide me with boots, and a bag,—'tis no joke,—
  Your fortune I'll make then straightway."

PUSS IN BOOTS.

PUSS PRESENTING THE RABBITS TO THE KING.

Puss baited his bag with parsely and bread,
  And away to the warren he hied,
Where he laid himself down as if he was dead,
  And some very young rabbits he spied.

One entered the bag, Puss pull'd at the string,
  The rabbit was kill'd in a trice;
Puss said this fine game I'll take to the king,
  I'm sure he will say it is nice.

PUSS IN BOOTS.

PUSS CATCHING THE PATRIDGES.

Next to a wheat field Grimalkin repair'd,
And there two fine patridges caught;
These he took to the king who kindly inquired
From whence the fine present was brought.

"From the Marquis Carabas, great Monarch," said he,
"These birds and the rabbits I bring."
They both were accepted, and Puss in hign glee,
Received a reward from the king.

PUSS IN BOOTS.

PUSS TALKING TO THE REAPERS.

The king took a journey, his kingdom to view,
With his daughter so fine and so gay,
What happen'd then, I will tell unto you,
To my tale therefore listen, I pray.

Puss ran to a cornfield, to the reapers he said,
"When the king comes, these words you repeat:
"To the Marqais Carabis these fields all belong,"
Or I'll chop you as fine as minced meat.

PUSS IN BOOTS.

PUSS BOWING TO THE OGRE.

To an Ogre's grand castle, Grimalkin now went,
Which was open'd by servants so gay,
"Is his highness, the Ogre, at home," said he,
"For my business is urgent to-day."

The Ogre received him with kindness, and now
Puss enter'd the castle so gay,
When making a low and reverend bow,
He march'd to the parlour straightway.

PUSS IN BOOTS.

THE OGRE TURNED INTO A LION.

"'Tis thought mighty Ogre, by all in the nation
That miraculous power you possess;
The power when you please of complete transformation,
This a miracle is, and no less.'

"To convince you, 'tis true," the Ogre replied,
"I will change myself now in your sight:"
He did so,—a lion he now roars by his side,
Which put the poor cat in a fright.

PUSS IN BOOTS.

PUSS CATCHING THE MOUSE.

"Mighty sir," said the cat, "such a change I must say,
I never expected to view;
Yet I venture to doubt, your pardon I pray,
If a mouse you could change yourself too."

"Doubt not," said the Ogre, "my power to do so,"
When a mouse he directly became,
On his victim Grimalkin immediately flew,
And sealed in an instant his doom.

PUSS IN BOOTS.

PUSS SHOWING IN THE KING AND PRINCESS.

The King and the Princess now arrived at the place,
But Puss who had travelled much faster,
Came out and invited them in with much grace,
In the name of the Marquis his master.

In a spacious saloon they sat themselves down,
Where a banquet was already spread,
And that day, PUSS IN BOOTS gained greater renown,
For the Marquis and Princess were wed.

Illustrations on this page are from "The Famous History of Tom Thumb, Wherein Is Declared His Marvellous Acts of Manhood," London, no date.

VI/ *Words of One Syllable*

SOME years ago a library and reading group published an age-grouped vocabulary as a guide to children's book authors. This "gimmick" was seized upon by many publishers, authors, teachers and librarians as an educational yardstick. A long list of books, particularly for pre-school and early grade-school children, was published that conformed to this anti-literary strait jacket. This supposedly novel fad is still in vogue to some extent. The principle espoused is that children of a given age can master only a limited number of words. The books and those publishers that confine themselves to this vocabulary make sure that the children do in fact stay limited.

This practice was old over one hundred years ago. It was more excusable at that time, when authors experimented with different approaches. Such attempts, however, did and do deprive children of the opportunity to "play with words," to enlarge their vocabularies to the full extent of their individual potential, and restricted them to expressing themselves monosyllabically.

Little Scenes for Good Boys

IN WORDS NOT EXCEEDING TWO SYLLABLES, WITH BEAUTIFUL ENGRAVINGS

London, Printed for the Booksellers, circa 1820

THE ROCKING HORSE.

This is a famous dashing steed, and he appears to have a very smart, active young rider. He has a firm and graceful seat, and has his reins well in hand. He rides too with a great deal of courage, although we must admit that his charger is not likely to swerve from the course which he wishes him to keep, nor, though going at full gallop, is there any danger of his being thrown, or run away with by the docile creature on which he is mounted.

CHARLES' NEW BOAT.

OUR young sailor has just launched his new vessel, and a very neat and trim one it is. The rigging is in good order, and the wind fills the spreading sails bravely. The grace and beauty of the bark seems greatly to delight Charles, as well as his two sisters, who have come to partake in the pleasure of the scene. I do not know what cargo the vessel has on board, but I think their is not much danger of her being wrecked, as she is not likely to sail far out of her master's care and sight.

THE FLOWER GARDEN.

What a pretty scene a flower garden affords! Roses, tulips, wall-flowers, and many others, alike pleasing to the sight and the smell. The little boy deserves to enjoy all the pleasure that the garden can procure him; for he is at work with his tools, his spade, his barrow, and his rolling stone, which shews a desire of making himself useful. I believe, too, he has kindly given his sister the rose at which she is smelling, and he will, I have no doubt, help the youngest in filling her basket.

THE PET DOG.

Stand up, Pompey! You are only half a soldier yet. You have got your gun in your hand, but we must put your helmet on besides, to make you complete. Poor Pompey! he is as peaceful and quiet as a lamb, and willing to do any thing that he can which he is told to do. The children round him seem kind and fond of him, and I trust they will not keep him standing long, because, though it may amuse them to see him play a trick or two, this posture is not easy to him.

VII/ *Robinsonades*

FOLLOWING its first appearance in 1719, Daniel Defoe's *Robinson Crusoe* was almost immediately compressed into adult and children's chapbook format. It was not only pirated, but inspired a school of literary adventure so multifarious as to give rise to a name of its own: "Robinsonades." These books were written in a similar vein, sometimes more or less clumsily disguised, at other times frankly imitative.

Swift's *Gulliver's Travels* (1726) was of a different genre. Though it also became a children's favorite, it did not suffer imitation or piracy in great numbers.

Of the many works inspired directly by Defoe, only Wyss's *Swiss Family Robinson* (1812) and Marryat's *Masterman Ready* (1841) deserve mention. This epoch of writing ended when Rousseau's romantic ideal of the "noble savage" was replaced by such documentary accounts as those of Livingstone and Stanley.

Children's adventure stories have always dealt with the individual conquest of the unknown wilderness. It will be interesting to see what form adventure stories for children will take as a result of electronically controlled team exploration. In former days a misadventure meant deprivation, starvation and misery over which man's spirit and endurance sometimes did triumph. Twentieth-century misadventure does not permit the hero to escape through stamina and faith. Miscalculation brings instant death.

1 Robinson Crusoe

THE SURPRISING LIFE AND MOST STRANGE ADVENTURES OF ROBINSON CRUSOE OF THE CITY OF YORK, MARINER

From John Ashton, "Chap-Books of the Eighteenth Century," London, Chatto & Windus, 1882

HE SETS SAIL ON HIS EVENTFUL VOYAGE.

THE WRECK.

ROBINSON AND XURY ESCAPING FROM THE MOORS.

HE KEEPS A RECORD OF TIME AND EVENTS

ADVENT OF FRIDAY.

ARRIVAL OF SAVAGES WITH CHRISTIAN PRISONER.

LANDING OF MUTINOUS CREW ON ISLAND.

2 Life and Adventures of Robinson Crusoe

GIVING AN ACCOUNT OF HIS SHIPWRECK AND SOLITARY LIFE ON AN UNINHABITED ISLAND

New Haven: S. Babcock, 1849

VIII/ *Humor and Riddles*

HUMOR, more than any other oral or literary style, is subject to fashion. What recently seemed uproariously funny is only mildly amusing now. The descent from drawing room and public house to the playground is rapid. What was bawdy and vulgar in one half of a century is the commonplace of the small fry in the next.

Riddles and conundrums have origins buried in the Middle East even before the time of the oracle at Delphi. The Rebus—letters and numbers added to and subtracted from illustrated nouns—was an adult craze in the eighteenth century. These forms found their way into chapbooks and later into the children's literature.

The only really new form of joke is the Limerick. It suddenly appeared in the late eighteenth century to reach full flowering at the hand of Edward Lear in the nineteenth. Even the whimsy of Lewis Carroll's "Alice" had a forerunner in "The World Turned Upside Down," a favorite subject of early chapbooks.

1 Jerry Diddle and His Fiddle

London: Printed by J. Catnach, 2 Monmouth Court, Seven Dials (no date)

IF YOU ARE BAD
I PRAY REFORM,

AND PRAISE WILL ALL
YOUR ACTS ADORN

JERRY DIDDLE
Bought a fiddle,
To play to little boys,
He wax'd his string,
And began to sing,
Youth is the time for joys.

HE went to a pig, and play'd a jig.
The pigs did grunt for joy,
Till the farmer came out,
And made a great rout,
Saying "Off, or I'll cane you, my boy."
He met an old woman to market a prancing,
He took out his fiddle, and set her a dancing.

SHE broke all her eggs,
And dirtied her butter;
At which her old husband
Began for to splutter.

Oh! then, said Jerry,
I'll soon make you merry.

AND the way with his fiddle he led,
The old man heard the tune,
As he sat in his room,
And danc'd on top of his head.

HE next met a barber,
With powder and wig,
He play'd him a tune,
And he shaved an old pig.

THEN up in his arms
He carried the boar,
And went to the ale-house,
To dance on the floor.

HE went to a fishwoman,
Tippling of gin,
When she like a top,
Began for to spin.

HE next met an old man,
With beard white and long,
Who laugh'd at poor Jerry,
And scoff'd at his song.

HIS name was Instruction,
The friend of the wise,
Who teaches good youth,
To win honor's prize.

HE broke Jerry's fiddle,
And taught him to read,
And told him that honor
Would daily succeed.

JERRY now is a lad
At school always true,
The joy of his friends,
And a pattern for you.

BE instructed by him,
To avoid folly's snare,
And your bosom thro' life,
Will escape every care.

2 The Gaping, Wide-Mouthed, Waddling Frog

British, probably 1823, publisher unknown

Command—Take this.

Question—What's this?

Answer.

Four Horses stuck in a bog.
Three Monkeys tied to a log.
Two Puddings'-ends that won't choke a Dog,
Nor a gaping, wide-mouthed, waddling Frog.

Command, Take this.—*Question*, What's this?

Answer. Nine Peacocks in the air;—
I wonder how they all got there:
You don't know, nor I don't care.
Eight Joiners in Joiners'-hall,
Working with their tools and all.
Seven Lobsters in a dish,
As good as any heart can wish.
Six Beetles against the wall,
Close to an old woman's apple-stall.
Five Puppies that loudly bawl,
And daily for their breakfast call.
Four Horses stuck in a bog.
Three Monkeys tied to a log.
Two Puddings'-ends that won't choke a dog.
Nor a gaping, wide-mouthed, waddling Frog.

Command, Take this.—*Question*, What's this?

Answer. Twelve Huntsmen, with horns and hounds,
Hunting over other men's grounds.
Eleven Ships sailing on the main,
Some bound for France, and some for Spain:
I wish them all safe back again.
Ten Comets in the sky, some low and some high.
Nine Peacocks in the air —I wonder how they all got there:
You don't know, nor I don't care.
Eight Joiners in Joiners'-hall, working with their tools and all.
Seven Lobsters in a dish, as good as any heart can wish.
Six Beetles against the wall, close to an old woman's apple-stall.
Five Puppies that loudly bawl, and daily for their breakfast call.
Four Horses stuck in a bog.
Three Monkeys tied to a log.
Two Puddings'-ends that won't choke a dog,
Nor a gaping, wide-mouthed, waddling Frog.

3 Grandmamma Easy's Old Dame Hicket and Her Wonderful Cricket

Boston: Brown, Bazin & Co. Nashua, N. H.; N. P. Greene & Co., circa 1840

There was one old Dame Hicket,
Had a wonderful Cricket,
That dwelt in a hole by the fender,
And when he came out
He would walk all about,
On his hind legs so tall and slender.
This so pleased the old Dame
That she gave him a name,
"Little Peter," it was, you must know;
And she fed him with crumbs
'Twixt her fingers and thumbs,
Before into his hole he did go.

When the evenings were long
He would sing a gay song,
And loudly out he would bellow,
Or as merry as a grig
Dance a lively jig;
Now was n't he a comical fellow?
Sometimes, too, 't is said,
He would stand on his head,
And swing his legs up in the air;
Then down he would pop,
And chirp, run and hop,
Just as if he was mad, I declare.

He 'd sit on a stool
Like a child at school,
Whilst the Dame she would read him a book;
And nod with his head
At each word she said,
As now he is doing, just look.
When the Dame took her snuff,
Which was often enough,
Politely she 'd hand him the box;
But the first thing he did,
Was to shut down the lid,
And then give it two or three knocks.

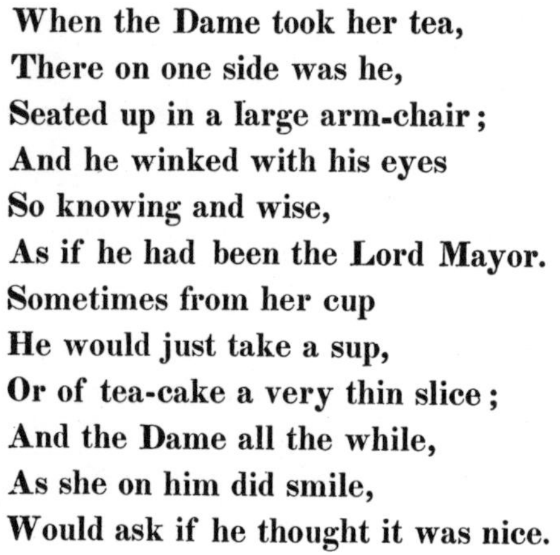

When the Dame took her tea,
There on one side was he,
Seated up in a large arm-chair;
And he winked with his eyes
So knowing and wise,
As if he had been the Lord Mayor.
Sometimes from her cup
He would just take a sup,
Or of tea-cake a very thin slice;
And the Dame all the while,
As she on him did smile,
Would ask if he thought it was nice.

But the Dame, one night,
Had a terrible fright,
For the Cricket he hopped on her nose.
She cried, "What 's there?"
When down went her chair,
And up in the air went her toes.
The Cricket did run,
When he saw this fun,
And quickly got right out of sight;
Whilst the Dame, with much pain,
Scrambled up once again,
And vowed she would kill him outright.

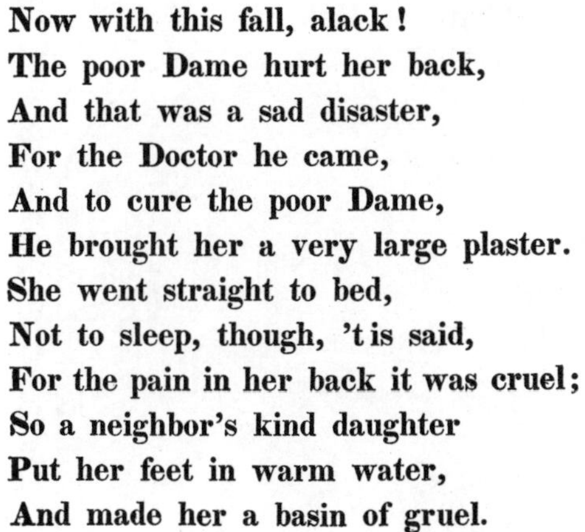

Now with this fall, alack!
The poor Dame hurt her back,
And that was a sad disaster,
For the Doctor he came,
And to cure the poor Dame,
He brought her a very large plaster.
She went straight to bed,
Not to sleep, though, 'tis said,
For the pain in her back it was cruel;
So a neighbor's kind daughter
Put her feet in warm water,
And made her a basin of gruel.

Now all the same day
She was in the same way,
And scarcely could hobble at all;
Whilst the Cricket, to tease,
Danced about at his ease,
And once again near made her fall.
This the dame so much vexed,
And sorely perplexed,
She'd have done with the Cricket forever,
So, as well as she could,
With a nail and some wood,
She stopped up the hole quite clever.

4 A Curious Hieroglyphick Bible

OR SELECT PASSAGES IN THE OLD AND NEW TESTAMENTS, REPRESENTED WITH EMBLEMATICAL FIGURES, FOR THE AMUSEMENT OF YOUTH

Published by T. Hodgson in George's-Court, London, 1789

Theſe three

as out of one praiſed and glorified God in the burning fiery

without being ſinged; ſaying, Bleſſed art thou, O Lord God of our Fathers, thy Name is worthy to be praiſed and exalted above all for ever.

Leviticus XXIII. *ver.* 3. 29

Six Days ſhall be done, but the ſeventh Day is the Sabbath of Reſt, an holy ye ſhall do no Work therein, it is the Sabbath of the Lord.

Six Days ſhall *Work* be done, but the ſeventh Day is the Sabbath of Reſt, an holy *Aſſembly*; ye ſhall do no Work therein, it is the Sabbath of the Lord.

HABAKKUK I. *ver.* 8. 71
Their
are ſwifter than the
and are more fierce
than the Evening
Their
are many,
and ſhall come from far; they ſhall
fly as the
haſting
to Meat.
Their *Horſes* are ſwifter than the *Leopards*, and are more fierce than the Evening *Wolves*: Their *Horſemen* are many, and ſhall come from far; they ſhall fly as the *Eagle* haſting to Meat.

St. LUKE II. *ver.* 16. 89
The Shepherds came with Haſte, and found
and
and the Babe lying in a
The Shepherds came with Haſte, and found *Mary* and *Joſeph*, and the Babe lying in a *Manger*.

5 A Whetstone for Dull Wits

OR A POESY OF NEW AND INGENIOUS RIDDLES

Of Merry Books this is the Chief,
'Tis as a purging Pill;
To carry off all heavy Grief
And make you laugh your Fill.

Q. A Wide Mouth, no ears nor eyes,
No scorching flames I feel—
Swallow more than may suffice
Full forty at a meal.

A. *It is an Oven.*

Q. A thing with a thundering breech
It weighing a thousand welly,
I have heard it roar
Louder than Guys wild boar,
They say it hath death in its belly.

A. *It is a Cannon.*

Q. To the green wood
Full oft it hath gang'd.
Yet yields us no good
Till decently hang'd.

A. *It is a hog fattened with Acorns, which makes good bacon when hanged a drying.*

Q. My back is broad, my belly is thin,
And I am sent to pleasure youth;
Where mortal man has never been
Tho' strange it is a naked truth.

A. *A Paper Kite which mounts the lofty air.*

6 The Puzzling Cap

British, circa 1780

Riddle XVII

WITHOUT a bridle or a saddle
Across a ridge I ride and straddle;
And ev'ry one, by help of me,
Tho' almost blind are made to see.
Then tell me, ev'ry pretty dame,
And witty Master, what's my name.

A Pair of Spectacles

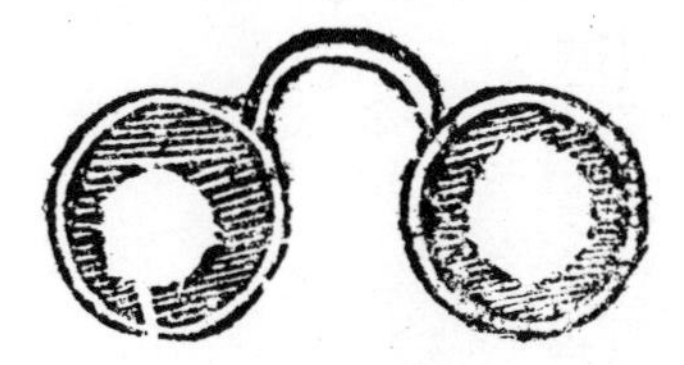

Riddle XX

THO' it be cold, I wear no cloaths,
The frost and snow I never fear;
I value neither shoes nor hose,
And yet I wander far and near:

My diet is for ever free,
I drink no cyder, port or sack;
What Providence doth send to me,
I neither buy, nor sell, nor lack.

A Fish

Riddle XXVI

PREFERMENT lately was bestow'd,
Upon a man tho' mean and small;
A thousand then about him flow'd,
Yet he return'd no thanks at all;
But yet their hands are ready still,
To help him with their kind good will.

A Man in a Pillory

7 A Collection of Birds and Riddles

BY MISS POLLY & MASTER TOMMY

York: J. Kendrew, Printer, Colliergate, circa 1825

The Hawk

THO' sharp thine eye and feathers fine
How cruel 'tis on Birds to dine!
But says the farmer with a sneer,
I wish I had more of them here;
If all loved corn, and none ate meat,
We too might soon want bread to eat.

Riddle

WHEN mortals are involv'd in ills,
I sing with mournful voice;
If mirth their hearts with gladness fills,
I celebrate their joys.
And as the lark with warbling throat,
Ascends upon the wing;
So I lift up my cheerful note,
And as I mount I sing.

Riddle

HOW many hundreds for my sake have died!
What frauds and villanies have not been tri'd?
And all the grandeur which my race adorns
Is like the Rose beset around with thorns.

IX/ *Books on Sports, Games and Pastimes*

AFTER the turn of the nineteenth century, boys and girls were encouraged to go out and play, to keep busy, to practice and exercise manual and scientific skills in addition to the purely moral and academic disciplines. Games, do-it-yourself pastimes and amusements, optical and aural illusions, simple electrical experiments and all manner of scientific magic became the subject of yet another new branch of children's literature. Today's Op Art is nothing more than a revival of the juvenile tricks of the early nineteenth century.

The *Imagerie Populaire* published penny prints of cutout soldiers, crèches, scenes and buildings, ranging from palaces and castles to farms. Towards the middle of the century these constructions required such skills and patience that I doubt if any contemporary plastic-hobby-kit practitioner could tackle them with any degree of success.

The scientific amusement books were largely based on a fifteenth-century compilation of chemical and mechanical formulae that had been pirated and reprinted through the centuries. As the new science turned to careful observation and classification of phenomena, the science of the alchemists became child's play.

1 Juvenile Games

FOR THE FOUR SEASONS

Edinburgh: Oliver & Boyd, High Street, 1823

Advertisement

THIS little Work contains a description of a great variety of GAMES suited to the FOUR SEASONS of the YEAR, and is intended solely for the amusement of Young Persons. As these games are perfectly free from any thing that can in the smallest degree injure the health or morals of youth, it is hoped they will be acceptable to the Public. A Work of this kind is calculated, in many respects, to be useful. Emulation, in any thing that is not bad, has always a good tendency; and if this laudable spirit is engendered at play, it will undoubtedly be retained, perhaps increased, in the pursuit of learning; by which the most beneficial effects may flow from it.

Nineholes

The Humming Ball

Games for Spring

Cup and Ball

Draughts

Games for Summer

Cat

Sliding

The Nuts

Scotch-Hoppers

Games for Autumn

Games for Winter

2 Girl's Own Book

BY MRS. CHILD

Boston: American Stationer's Company, 1837

The Hen Coop

Butterfly and Flowers

Shuttlecock and Battledoor

The Comical Concert

French and English

Blind Man's Buff

Jumping Rope

Swinging

Exercises with the Wand

La Grace

Cup and Ball

3 Juvenile Pastimes, In Verse

American, circa 1820

COME Boys and Girls, come out to play,
The moon doth shine, as bright as day,
Come with a whoop, come with a call,
Come with a good will, or not at all.

Marbles

AT Marbles, two or three can play,
At morning, noon, or close of day,
Plump goes the marble, with aim true,
Out from the ring it knocks a few.

Trap and Ball

I Spy Hi!

IN this play, the boys do choose
Those who for running are most us'd:
Now out they go, they spy, they hide,
If they can catch one, home they ride.

THIS play is quite innocent and useful, provided it is done off the pavement, or not in the time which should be devoted to study or business.

Skipping the Rope

SO sprightly o'er the verdant ground
See the skippers nimbly bound,
Round goes the rope, up jumps the boy
Th' occasion to them of much joy.

Bow and Arrow

BEND well your bow, your skill to try
Then shoot the target in the eye:
'Tis better thus to be employ'd
Than have the birds for nought destroy'd.

Flying the Kite

Foot Ball

UP goes the ball, now hit it well,
Who'll kick it next, is hard to tell
Take care you don't each other wound,
Nor make a tumble on the ground.

Ride in a Chair

CARRY young *Mary* safe and sound,
Or she will fall upon the ground:
How fine she rides! how pleas'd they are!
'Tis hard to tell which best do fare.

Rocking Horse

Swinging

THEIR time to pass in healthful play,
The boys and girls they swing away;
But do take care the rope be fast,
Ere a sad fall you catch at last.

Leap-Frog

The Hoop

The Jumping Rope

Blind Man's Buff

Archery

Ball

All illustrations on this page are from "The Boy's and Girl's Book of Sports," New York and Philadelphia, about 1835.

X/ *Periodicals*

PUBLISHERS of juvenile books were quick to learn that children could be snared into subscribing to books even before they were published. This practice led to the publication, in 1788, of *The Juvenile Magazine*, the first British periodical for children. Puzzle pages with solutions given in succeeding issues, letters to the editor, and similar devices encouraged children to send in their subscriptions and assured the publisher of a continuous guaranteed market.

The *Juvenile Miscellany*, published in Boston in 1827, *Peter Parley's Magazine* and many others swelled the competitive ranks of such periodicals in the United States. They were particularly attractive to the children of settlers far from cities and libraries. They were also excellent sales media for toys and so-called "premiums" that stimulated a substantial mail-order trade from otherwise inaccessible juvenile customers.

Not until the middle of the century did such periodicals begin to attract authors of note and to make an effort to present literary fare comparable to the children's books of their day. Dickens, Twain and others eventually came to be occasional contributors to such magazines as *St. Nicholas*.

1 The Juvenile Magazine

OR AN INSTRUCTIVE AND ENTERTAINING MISCELLANY FOR YOUTH OF BOTH SEXES

For January, 1788; J. Marshall and Co., London

Answers and Acknowledgments to Correspondents

To the LADY who inquires "whether this Magazine is designed for different ages?"—The Editor answers, That it is chiefly intended for young people, from SEVEN to FOURTEEN years of age; and, consequently, that tales of *Gallantry*, *Love*, *Courtship* or *Marriage* cannot be admitted; nor any in which the conduct or foibles of a PARENT are treated disrespectfully, or set in a ridiculous point of view.

The PUBLISHERS *beg leave to say, that they hoped by publishing this Magazine* to unite the talents *of those friends who had kindly furnished them with little tracts for the Instruction and Entertainment of Young Minds, and to invite contributions from those who, though they possess abilities, have not leisure nor inclination to write a volume.—A few have assisted in this Month's Magazine; but as others withhold their assistance till a future Number, the Publishers trust that the Work will improve; and that their First Number will be the worst.*

The Editor's Address to Her Young Readers

My Young Readers,

The very great partiality I entertain for youth, has induced me to engage in a plan, which I flatter myself will be productive not only of your *present* amusement, but of your *future* welfare. . . .

There are, without doubt among you, some who are, from various circumstances, deprived of a tender parent, or friend, to correct their little foibles, and to guide them with propriety in the path of life they are destined to tread; to *such*, the Editor of the *Juvenile Magazine* may not prove a useless correspondent; should you, my young friends, at any time perceive an *unruly passion* or *habit* intruding, or a *situation* in which you are at a loss to conduct yourselves, by addressing a letter to the *Editor*, at *Mr. Marshall*'s, you will be furnished, in the next Magazine, with that advice which may enable you to *overcome* the one, and accommodate yourselves to the other.

Those young persons who wish to contribute to the *Juvenile Magazine* by any literary production, will have that attention paid to their performances, which their abilities, and the goodness of their intentions may merit.

THE

Juvenile Magazine;

OR, AN

INSTRUCTIVE *and* ENTERTAINING

MISCELLANY

FOR

YOUTH of BOTH SEXES.

For *January* 1788

Embelliſhed with Two Prints; L'ENFANT DOCILE; and the SILLY BOY.

CONTENTS.

PRINTED and PUBLISHED by and for

J. Marshall and Co.

Aldermary Church-Yard, Bow-Lane, Cheapſide, LONDON.

To whom COMMUNICATIONS *(Poſt paid)* are requeſted to be addreſſed; and by whom any Hints for the Improvement of the Publication, will be thankfully received.

2 The Juvenile Miscellany

FOR THE INSTRUCTION AND AMUSEMENT OF YOUTH

John Putnam, Boston, 1830

Instruction from the Mouth of a Child

"MAMMA," said little Lucy B., "my Sunday School teacher told me that this world is only a place in which God lets us live a little while, in order that we may have time to prepare for a better world. But, mother, I don't see anybody preparing. I see you preparing to go into the country; and when I make a visit to aunt Eliza, I see her preparing to come into Boston. But I don't see anybody preparing to go to heaven. If every body want to go there, why don't they try to get ready?"

Lapland Family Returning From the Coast

IT is not incompatible with the great arrangements by which the universe has been created, and is supported, to believe that the rein-deer has been specially bestowed upon the inhabitants of the polar regions, as an improvement of their necessary lot, in the same way that the locality of the camel has been fixed in the sandy and stony deserts of Asia and Africa. The poor Laplander knows the value of the faithful creature which affords him food, clothing, and the means of transport; and he offers his homage of thanksgiving to the Great Author of nature, who has given him this companion of his wanderings. Whether the native of the polar regions hunt the wild deer amidst the icy mountains,—be hurried by his aid across the frozen wastes,—or wander with his family and his herds, till the long winter begins, almost without any gradation, to succeed the short summer,—the lives of the Laplander and of the rein-deer are inseparably united.

3 Merry's Museum

Peter Parley's New Stories, "Merry's Museum," June, 1842

Smelling

I PROPOSE to give my readers some remarks upon the five senses; and I shall begin with smelling. The seat of this sense is the nose, and the chief instrument by which it operates is a soft membrane, lining the interior of the nostrils. This is covered over with an infinite number of organs, too delicate to be seen by the naked eye, called the *olfactory nerves*. As the brain is the seat of the mind, these nerves extend to it, and convey to that organ every impression that is made upon them. The nerves are like sentinels or messengers stationed in all parts of the body, whose duty it is to communicate to the seat of power—to the brain, and thus to the intellect—everything that happens to the body. Thus, if you pinch your finger, or stub your toe, or put your hand in the fire, or taste of an apple, the nerves carry the story to the mind.

So it is with the olfactory nerves; they have the power of perceiving what effluvia is in the air, and they tell the mind of it.

However others may feel, I maintain that the nose is, on the whole, a good thing.

Ingenious Contrivances of Nature

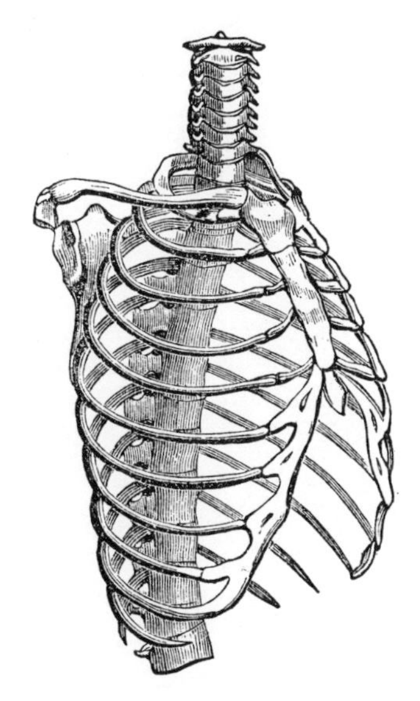

The human spine

A Shop-Keeper in New York, the other day, stuck upon his door the following laconic advertisement: "*A boy wanted.*" On going to his shop, the next morning, he beheld a smiling urchin in a basket, with the following pithy label: "*Here it is.*"

The Sense of Taste

THE tongue, which has so much to do with talking, has a good deal to do with tasting. It is indeed one of the chief instruments by which the sensation of taste is experienced. The palate is also another organ of importance in the perception of taste.

It will be perceived that the saliva of the mouth is one great cause of all taste. When the tongue is rendered dry by disease, or any other circumstance, the sense of taste is either imperfect or lost. The pressure of the tongue against the surface of the mouth seems also to be important in producing the sense of taste; for if you put anything into your mouth, and hold it open, the sensation is hardly produced. It is from the effect of this pressure that the act of chewing and swallowing gives us so much pleasure.

Old Age

HERE is a picture of an old man, walking in the woods, and a little bird, on the tree, seems to be speaking to him. What do you think the little bird says to the old man? I will try to tell you. Thus speaks the little bird:

"Come, good old man, and speak to me,
For I am young and thou art old;
Full many a year hath passed o'er thee,
And many a tale of wisdom told.

Give me thy counsel, aged wight;
For here the hawk doth prowl by day,
And many a cruel owl by night—
Seeking on little birds to prey."

Now the bird here shows good sense. Instead of avoiding old people, children should always love to be with them, and should always treat them with kindness, attention and respect. Old people are usually very fond of children, and they can tell them many pretty tales, and many curious things they have seen.

XI/ *Books That Teach*

IT was fashionable, even in the early days of children's book publishing, to imply the presence of "education" in the promotion of the new literature. At the same time an attempt was made to introduce some play and entertainment into learning. Pestalozzi, and later Froebel, had begun experiments in "play-learning" and the "kindergarten method." Classicism was on the wane. While discipline was still rigid, as "Little Jack Jingle" can testify, the approach to learning and instruction was changing. In their own pedantic ways, the nineteenth-century school masters and mistresses were greatly influenced by the new juvenile literature—and vice versa.

The instruction offered in the following sampling of school texts attempts to interest children and to make learning less of a chore. The non-scholastic works try to teach in their own way, expanding the horizon of children, informing in an entertaining manner. These were the first steps in the democratization of education, making information and literacy available to middle- and lower-class children. Occupations from barbering to whaling and farming, as well as botany, zoology, and geography, were now deemed suitable subjects for popular education, replacing exclusive preoccupation with classical, mythological and moral subjects.

Much of the information offered was carelessly compiled and misleading. Many of the writers themselves were scarcely educated; others had peculiar pedagogic ideas, such as the author of "Little Frank's Almanac," a curious little book which stands out among its fellows. It seems reasonably certain that few of its readers ever did get the days of the week straight.

"New" has always been a catchword in education. With the discovery that parental feelings of guilt and inadequacy could be turned into a potent sales lever, "new methods" of turning little dunces into geniuses were quickly exploited commercially. The "new math" of 1816 consisted of "Marmaduke Multiply." Putting the multiplication table and the ABC's to rhyme supposedly helped memory where before it had been entirely encouraged by the rod.

1 Jack Jingle

London: J. Catnach, 2 Monmouth Court, Seven Dials (no date)

LITTLE Jack Jingle,
  Played truant at school,
They made his bum tingle
For being a fool;
He promised no more
Like a fool he would look
But be a good boy and attend to his book.

HERE sulky Sue,
  What shall we do.
Turn her face to the wall,
  Till she comes to;
If that should fail,
  A touch with the cane
Will do her good,
  When she feels the pain.

LITTLE Jack Jingle,
  Went to court Suky Shingle,
Says he, shall we mingle
  Our toes in the bed;
Fye! Jacky Jingle,
  Says little Suke Shingle,
We must try to mingle,
  Our pence for some bread.

SUKY you shall be my wife,
  And I'll tell you why;
I have got a little pig,
  And you have got a sty;
I have got a dun cow,
  And you can make good cheese,
Suky will you have me?
  Say yes, if you please.

2 The Good Child's Illustrated Alphabet

OR FIRST BOOK

London: Published by Ryle & Paul, 2 & 3, Monmouth Court, Seven Dials (no date)

Was an Archer,
Who shot at a frog.

Was a Butcher,
And kept a great dog.

Was a Captain,
All covered with lace.

Was a Drunkard
And had a red face.

Was an Esquire,
With insolent brow.

Was a Farmer, And
Followed the plough.

Was a Gamester,
Who had but ill-luck.

Was a Huntsman,
And hunting a buck.

Was an Inn-keeper,
Who loved to bouse.

Was a joiner,
And built up a house.

Was King William,
Once governed this land.

Was a Lady, who
Had a white hand.

Was a Miser,
And hoarded up gold.

Was a Nobleman,
Gallant and bold.

Was an Oyster-wench,
And went about town.

Was a Parson, and
Wore a black gown.

Was a Queen,
Who was fond of flip.

Was a Robber,
And wanted a whip.

Was a Sailor,
Who spent all he got.

Was a Tinker,
And mended a pot.

Was a Usurer,
A miserly elf.

Was a Vinter, who
Drank all himself.

Was a Watchman,
And guarded the door.

Was Expensive,
And so became poor.

Was a Youth,
Who did not love school.

Was a Zany,
A silly old fool.

3 The Tragical Death of an Apple Pie

WHO WAS CUT TO PIECES AND EATEN BY TWENTY-FIVE GENTLEMEN, WITH WHOM ALL LITTLE PEOPLE OUGHT TO BE ACQUAINTED

London: Printed by J. Paul & Co., 2 & 3 Monmouth

A	B	C	D
An Apple-pie.	Bit it.	Cut it.	Dealt it.

E	F	G	H
Did eat it.	Fought for it.	Got it.	Had it.

J	K	L	M
Join'd for it.	Kept it.	Long'd for it.	Mourned for it.

N	O	P	Q
Nodded at it.	Open'd it.	Peeped into it.	Quartered it.

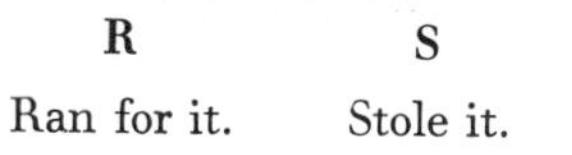

R	S	T	V
Ran for it.	Stole it.	Took it.	View'd it.

W
Wanted it.

XYZ and &
All wished for
a piece in hand.

AN apple pie when it looks nice,
Would make one long to have a slice,
And if its taste should prove so too,
I fear one slice would scarcely do,
So to prevent my asking twice,
Pray mamma, cut a good large slice.

AT last they every one agreed,
Upon the apple pie to feed;
But as there seem'd to be so many,
Those who were last might not have any,
Unless some method there was taken
That every one might have their bacon,

THEY all agreed to stand in order,
Around the apple pie's fine border,
Take turn as they in hornbook stand
From great A down to &,
In equal parts the pie divide,
As you may see on the other side.

A curious Discourse that passed between the Twenty-five Letters at dinner time.

A	1.	Says **A**, give me a good large slice.
B	2.	Says **B**, a little bit but nice.
C	3.	Says **C**, cut me a piece of crust.
D	4.	Take it, says **D**, 'tis dry as dust.
E	5.	Says **E**, I'll eat it fast, who will?
F	6.	Says **F**, I vow I'll have my fill.
G	7.	Says **G**, give it me both good and great.
H	8.	Says **H**, a little bit I hate.
I	9.	Says **I**, I love the juice the best.
K	10.	And **K**, the very same confess'd.
L	11.	Says **L**, there's nothing more I love.
M	12.	Says **M**, it makes your teeth to move.
N	13.	**N** notic'd what the other said,
O	14.	**O**, others plates with grief survey'd.
P	15.	**P** prais'd the cook up to the life.
Q	16.	**Q** quarrell'd because he'd a bad knife.
R	17.	Says **R**, it runs short I'm afraid.
S	18.	**S**, silent sat and nothing said.
T	19.	**T**, thought that talking might lose time.
U	20.	**U** understood it at meals a crime.
W	21.	**W** wish'd there had been a quince in.
X	22.	Says **X**, those cooks there's no convincing.
Y	23.	Says **Y**, I'll eat, let others wish.
Z	24.	**Z** sat as mute as any fish.
&	25.	While **&** he lick'd the dish.

4 The Golden Pippin

London: Printed by J. Catnach, 2 Monmouth Court, Seven Dials

A

Was an Arch Boy.

B

A Beauty was.

C

A comely Wench but Coy.

D

A Dainty Lass.

E

Loved Eggs, and eat his Fill.

F

Was full and fat.

G

Had Grace and wit at will.

H

Wore A Gold Lace Hat.

I

Stands for little Jackys name.

K

For Kitty Fair.

L

Loved learning & got fame.

M

Was his Mother dear.

N

Was naughty & oft crying.

O

An Only Child.

P
Was pretty Peggy sighing.

Q
Was a Quaker mild.

R
Was Rude & in disgrace.

S
Stands for Sammy Still.

T
For ever talked a-pace.

V
Was fond of Veal.

W
He watched the house & hall.

X
Does like a Cross appear.

Y
A Youth well shaped & tall.

Z
Whips up the Rear.

Let all good children come to me
And I'll teach them their ABC.

A	*A*	J	*J*	S	*S*
B	*B*	K	*K*	T	*T*
C	*C*	L	*L*	U	*U*
D	*D*	M	*M*	V	*V*
E	*E*	N	*N*	W	*W*
F	*F*	O	*O*	X	*X*
G	*G*	P	*P*	Y	*Y*
H	*H*	Q	*Q*	Z	*Z*
I	*I*	R	*R*		

& which stands for and

5 Mrs. Lovechild's Golden Present

FOR ALL GOOD LITTLE BOYS AND GIRLS; DECORATED WITH WOOD CUTS

York: Printed by J. Kendrew, Colliergate

My little children, pray attend
The admonitions of a friend,
Who places here before your view,
The boon of vice and virtue too;
All who are good the Orange share,
The rod no naughty boy shall spare.

A,
For the Apple, which was bought at the fair.

B,
For a Blockhead, who ne'er shall go there.

C,
For a Cauliflower, white as a curd.

D,
For a Duck, a very fine bird.

E,

For an Eagle, that soar'd in the skies.

F,

For a Farmer, rich, honest, and wise.

G,

Was a Gentleman, void of all care.

H,

Was the Hound, that run down the hare.

I,

Was an Indian, sooty and dark.

K,

For the Key, that lock'd up the park.

L,

Was a Lark, that soar'd in the air.

M,

Was a Mole, that ne'er could get there.

6 Marmaduke Multiply

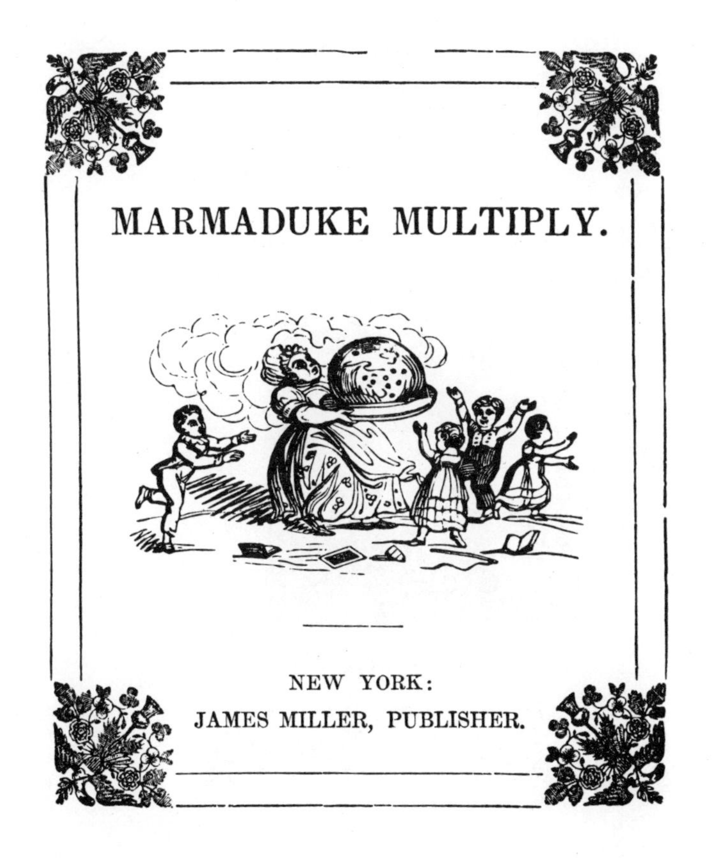

6

Twice 4 are 8.

Your bonnet is not straight.

20

3 times 6 are 18.

How long they keep me waiting.

13

Twice 11 are 22.

Mister, can you mend my shoe?

24

3 times 10 are 30.

My face is very dirty.

7 American Pictorial Primer

Philip J. Cozans, Publisher, 116 Nassau Street, New York, circa 1825

This is an Elephant. See, he is eating off a plate. The little boy is not afraid of him, for he is a very harmless animal. The Elephant is the largest animal in the world.

date	**left**	**dine**	**bone**
fade	**belt**	**five**	**bolt**
lade	**hemp**	**mile**	**tone**
mate	**bell**	**hive**	**hone**
lake	**peck**	**pine**	**bold**
gale	**pest**	**dive**	**mode**

PICTORIAL PRIMER. 23

IDLE MARY.

OH Mary, this will never do!
This work is sadly done, my dear,
And then so little of it too!
You have not taken pains, I fear.

8 The Holiday A B C Book

Publisher and date unknown, circa 1830

BENEVOLENCE.

BENNY, when the cripple knocks,
Brings the money from his box.
Bill and Bessy, by the table,
Say, "To give *we* are not able;
But, whoe'er the poor befriends,
To the Lord his money lends."

FRANK is drowning! Shall we fly,
And for help, distracted, cry?
"No," says Fred, amazing cool,
"Stop and learn this simple rule,
By the wise well understood,
'All is safe with *Fortitude*.'"

MARY cries, "Behold your queen!"
Milla adds, with sober mien,
"Royalty beneath the trees,—
Mike, go down upon your knees!"
Mike and Moses bow together
To old Tray, with hat and feather.

NEATNESS.

NELLY, with her brush and broom,
Makes a very tidy room;
Nancy is no careless slut,—
All her drawers are nicely shut
Both these little girls, you see,
Are as neat as neat can be.

WICKEDNESS.

WALTER WADE and Willie Grey
Break the holy Sabbath day.
While the bell for church doth toll,
Walter takes his fishing-pole;
Wicked Willie says, "Ring louder!
Guess the *old bell* wants some chowder."

9 The Picture Alphabet

OR CHILD'S A,B,C

Seventh series, No. 1. Portland, Me.: Bailey & Noyes, circa 1830

A  Axe.

  Bat

C 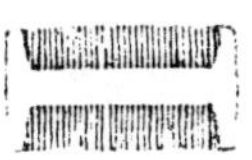 Comb.

D  Dish

E  Egg

F  Fan.

V  Vice

W 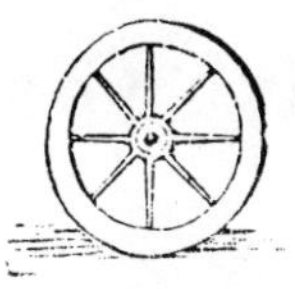 Wheel

X  Xerxes

Y  Youth.

Z  Ze-
bra.

FIGURES.

1 2 3 4 5 6 7 8 9 0

10 Pond's Murray's Grammar

IMPROVED EDITION

Worcester: Published by Dorr, Howland and Co., 1836

A man drinking.

HEAR the exclamations of this poor drunkard, and you will have an example of all the *tenses* of verbs. "*I drink,*" he says, in the *present* tense. "*I despised ardent spirit once;*" and here he speaks in the *imperfect* tense. "*I have ruined my character,*" he says, in the *perfect* tense. "*I had drank too much before I came in here;*" and this is the *pluperfect* tense. "*I shall repent of my folly,*" he cries, using the *first future* tense. "At the rate I have drank since I began in the morning," continues the deluded victim of the bottle, "*I shall have drunk* a quart at noon;" and here he uses the *second future* tense. Compare this with the lesson, and you will understand all the variations of the tenses.

11 Little Frank's Almanac

TO SHOW LITTLE BOYS AND GIRLS THEIR PLAY DAYS

Concord: John F. Brown, 1837

THIS curious little book, and the extraordinary information it contains, stands out among its fellows in my collection. The text, here reproduced in part, speaks for itself.—A.A.

FRANK says, if I play twelve hours and sleep twelve hours, that is, twenty-four hours, then is a whole day gone; and seven such days make a week; but, Emily does not know the names of all the days, and I shall now teach her on my own plan. So bring your cricket again, Emily, and call these names over after me, that I am going to show you. First, say Sunday Owl—Monday Falcon—Tuesday Quail—Wednesday Hoopoe—Thursday Vulture—Friday Avoset—Saturday Goose.

SUNDAY is the first day of the week.

OWL is the first Bird in our Book.

The Owl cannot look at the Sun, and therefore you will remember he is for Sunday. This day is also called the Lord's Day, and the Sabbath and the First Day.

MONDAY is the second day of the week.

FALCON is the second Bird in our Book.

The Falcon is a hunting bird and always flies as fast on Monday, as on other days.

TUESDAY is the third day of the week.

QUAIL is the third Bird in our Book.

The Quail is a pretty bird and is come off her nest on Tuesday. Now always remember the Quail on Tuesday, because she is next to the Falcon.

WEDNESDAY is the fourth day of the week.

HOOPOE is the fourth bird in our book.

The Hoopoe trims her crest on Wednesday, and wishes to look fine, for this is the middle day of the week, and she is going to a wedding.

THURSDAY is the fifth day of the week.

VULTURE is the fifth bird in our book.

The Vulture gets very hungry on Thursday, and will devour all kinds of dead animals. Thursday afternoon is a Play-Day.

FRIDAY is the sixth day of the week.

AVOSET is the sixth bird in our book.

The Avoset lives on fish, and you see he has a long bill to catch them. Friday is fish day, every one loves fried fish, and all catholics eat fish on Friday.

SATURDAY is the seventh day of the week.

GOOSE is the seventh bird in our book.

The poor Goose may be killed on Saturday, because they want her feathers to put into a bed; and when the bed is made you may lay down, for it is Saturday night, and you are tired.

Illustration from "Guess Again, or The Amusing Riddler," Philadelphia, Fisher and Brother, no date.

12 Life on the Farm

IN AMUSING RHYME

New York: Kiggins & Kellogg, 123 & 125 William Street, circa 1840

THE cock is crowing,
The cows are lowing,
The ducks are quacking,
Jane's tongue is clacking,
The geese are gabbling,
The brook is babbling,
Oh, deary me, what a noise.

THE bees all are humming,
Little George is drumming,
Moll water is splashing,
Old Joe is thrashing,
Little Joe is yelling,
Jim a tree is felling,
Was there ever such a noise?

TOM his scythe is whetting,
Old Susette is fretting,
The pigs they are squeaking
The barn-door is creaking,
Old Peter is talking,
The parrot is mocking,
Who can endure such a noise?

THE dull ass is braying,
The black horse is neighing,
The baby is squalling,
The nurse she is bawling,
The horn it is sounding,
The hammer is pounding,
The sheep are baa-baaing,
And the boys ha-haing,
Mercy on us what a noise!

ROBIN-redbreast is singing,
The dinner-bell's ringing,
The swallows are twittering,
The girls they are tittering,
The old cat is mewing,
The cook she is tewing,
The watch-dog is howling,
Old Towser is growling,
I'm most crazy with the noise!

THE grindstone is turning,
And Nabby is churning,
Goody Dobson is preaching,
The peacock is screeching,
I can not live in such a noise!

13 What Is Veal?

FROM JUVENILE POEMS

A. R. Merrifield, Northampton, 1841

WILLIAM asked how veal was made,
His little sister smiled,
It grew in foreign climes, she said,
And call'd him silly child.

ELIZA, laughing at them both,
Told, to their great surprise,
The meat cook boiled to make the broth,
Once lived, had nose and eyes;

NAY, more, had legs, and walked about;
William in wonder stood,
He could not make the riddle out,
But begged his sister would.

WELL, brother, I have had my laugh,
And you shall have yours now,
Veal, when alive, was call'd a calf—
Its mother was a cow.

14 Elton's Pictorial A.B.C.

EMBELLISHED WITH 230 ENGRAVINGS, OR, ILLUSTRATED NOUNS

New York: T. W. Strong, Publisher, 98 Nassau-Street, and 64 Cornhill, Boston, 1848

Ap-ple.
Arch.
A-corn.
Ar-row.
A-vo-set.
Adze.
An-chor.
Axe.
Boy.
Book.
Ba-by.
Bar-rel.
Bud.

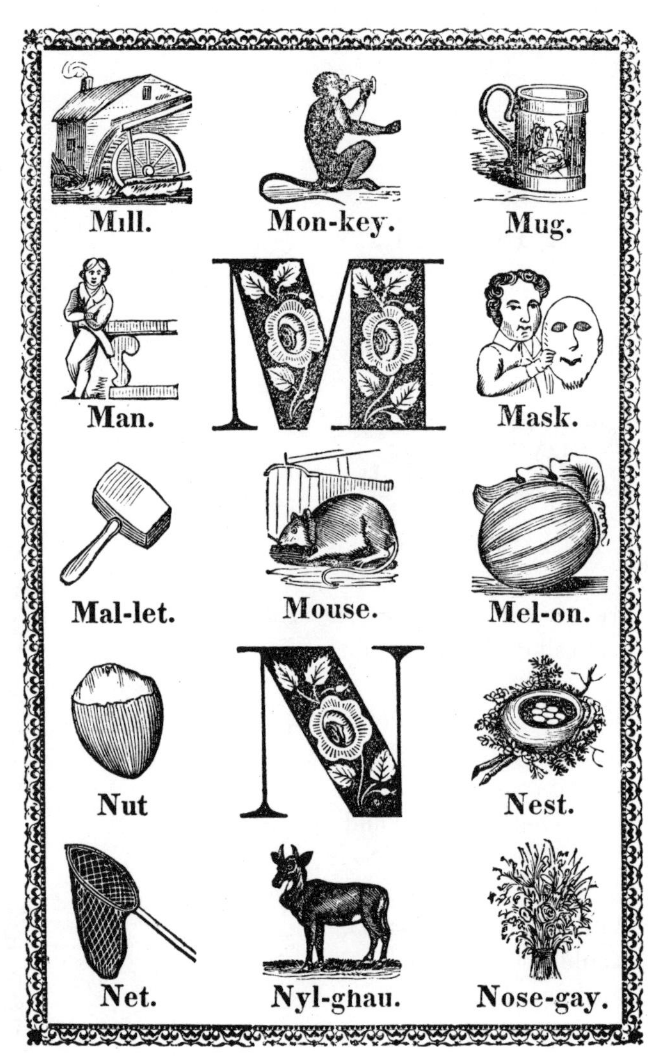
Mill.
Mon-key.
Mug.
Man.
Mask.
Mal-let.
Mouse.
Mel-on.
Nut
Nest.
Net.
Nyl-ghau.
Nose-gay.